As the man [...] tol and swung it in a short arc, ending on the swarthy man's temple. A dull crunch was drowned out by the clatter of the train's wheels. Joe Haskell fell heavily, stumbling as he tried to step over the broken seat.

Slocum lowered his six-shooter and reached out with his left hand. The man's grimy collar gave a good enough grip for Slocum to push Haskell toward the open window. The man's head stuck out as Slocum lowered himself into the good seat facing the broken one.

"Wha—" Haskell struggled as the hot air cut at his face and hot cinders thrown back from the engine burned his skin. Jerking harder, he tried to duck back into the car. Slocum rammed the barrel of his six-gun into the man's gut.

"Never expected to see me again, did you?" asked Slocum. "You shot at my back and thought I was dead."

"I never, I mean, I—"

"You missed," Slocum said coldly. "And you owe me fifty dollars."

JAKE LOGAN

SLOCUM AND THE BEAR LAKE MONSTER

JOVE BOOKS, NEW YORK

SLOCUM AND THE BEAR LAKE MONSTER

A Jove Book / published by arrangement with
the author

PRINTING HISTORY
Jove edition / February 1996

The Putnam Berkley World Wide Web site address is
http://www.berkley.com

ISBN: 0-515-11806-0

A JOVE BOOK®
Jove Books are published by The Berkley Publishing Group,
200 Madison Avenue, New York, New York 10016.
JOVE and the "J" design are trademarks
belonging to Jove Publications, Inc.

PRINTED IN THE UNITED STATES OF AMERICA

10 9 8 7 6 5 4 3 2 1

1

The Union Pacific passenger car rocked from side to side, throwing John Slocum around just enough to make sleeping on the hard, wooden seat impossible. He pushed back his tall, black Stetson and wiped his face with a sweat-drenched bandanna. Slocum reached over to shut the window that was letting in soot from the engine and the dust whipping across the hot Utah plains. The train had rattled through soaring mountains and high passes still powdered with snow all the way from Cheyenne and was now on a stretch running to Devils Gate and, beyond that, to the tiny town of Corinne and the famous Promontory Summit. For three years, since '69, the tracks had connected from Saint Louis all the way out to Oakland.

Slocum spat dust from his mouth and shook his hat off, sending a new cloud of grit through the car. He had no clear destination in mind. Leaving Cheyenne had been necessary after a bloody disagreement over a poker hand in the aptly named Four Aces Saloon. Slocum closed his eyes and tried to banish the images still flashing through his mind, even after almost three days: the gambler, dressed all in black, clanking from carrying so many hideout guns and knives; the ace he had clumsily dropped.

Slocum's fingers tapped lightly on the butt of the ebony-handled Colt Navy thrust into his cross-draw holster. With most cowboys, it wouldn't have mattered. With Slocum, it did. The gambler had been awkward when he slipped the extra ace into his hand to give himself the four aces. And he had been slow getting to the derringer stuffed into his vest pocket. Slocum was neither awkward nor slow. He had drawn and cut the gambler down with the first shot.

But how was he to know the gambler had so many friends in the casino? Three more ended up carrying bullets from John Slocum's six-gun. And one of them was hurt badly enough that he might soon join his gambling friend in the grave.

"And friends have friends, all sporting shotguns, six-shooters, and bad attitudes," Slocum muttered to himself. Cheyenne had grown uncomfortably dangerous for him, making a quick trip out of town necessary for his continued good health. Slocum stretched his aching muscles and leaned back, watching the desert country roll past at a steady clip. Tiring quickly of this, he turned to the passenger car and studied the other riders.

Across the aisle from where he sat alone, Slocum saw a man dressed in a fine coat sporting dark red velvet tab collars and decked out in gold rings with expensive watch chains dangling across a brocade vest. He pored over a stack of legal papers, all fluttering noisily in the hot wind blowing in the window. The man's eyes weren't always on the papers, though. Slocum saw the sly glances he cast from time to time to the man sitting opposite him, reading a book.

Finally, as if by accident, the well-dressed man let one sheet of paper slip from his fingers. It fluttered away crazily, carried by the wind. He made a sudden grab for it, causing the other man to drop his book and look up.

"Sorry, sir," the dandy said, retrieving his sheet of paper.

"I did not mean to intrude. I merely wanted to go over these land deeds."

"Deeds?" inquired the gentleman with the book.

Slocum kept from laughing. The dandy started discussing the gold find of the century and how he held the deeds to the land. The rest of the tale unfolded in snippets, as if the mark had to pry every detail from the peacock. Before long, the two sat side by side, going over the deeds. Slocum knew it wouldn't be much longer before serious negotiation started for the worthless pieces of paper.

He shook his head, marveling at how easy a clever confidence man removed surplus money from an unsuspecting man's wallet.

At the far end of the car, a game of three card monte proceeded, the mark never quite understanding why he lost when it was obvious where the queen lay. More for his own amusement than for any good reason, Slocum began pairing the men in the car, figuring out who worked together to extract money from the legitimate travelers. The land swindler across from him had no obvious accomplice. Two others, working a variant of the pigeon drop, had circled around the portly gentleman sitting between them as if they were vultures finding fresh carrion.

Slocum began to think everyone in the car worked some angle, trying to swindle the others—including even the ones doing the hoodwinking. Thieves stealing from thieves. Slocum liked the notion so much he chuckled to himself.

When they ran out of greenhorns, they had to skin each other. Slocum started to pull his hat down over his eyes to try to sleep again when he saw the three card monte artist moving away from his mark, having cleaned the young man out, and going to a dapper man, small and scholarly looking. When the cardsharp sat down, the man took off his spectacles and wiped them clean. The expression on his face was one of interest in the flashing cards being dropped on the large piece of cardboard spread over the gambler's knees.

Slocum had no interest in protecting the dapper man's money. What drew his attention was the lovely young lady seated next to him. She was slender and possessed a pale, oval face that reminded Slocum of pictures put on display in a photographer's studio. Every line was perfect, and her gray eyes danced with intelligence. She patted a strand of blond hair back under her hat when a particularly hot gust blew in the open window beside her traveling companion. The small man, who Slocum thought looked like a professor, hardly noticed, so intent was he on the cards flipping to and fro on the gambler's lapboard.

"This one," Slocum heard the man say, a stubby finger pressing down into the back of a bent and grimy playing card.

"Why, you're a quick study," congratulated the gambler dealing the three cards. "That's a whole two bits I lost to you. I need to make it back. Want to double the bet?"

"I should say so!" exclaimed the professor.

The dapper man won again. The card shuffling went on, the three card monte dealer seeming more and more agitated that the professor managed to win every time by picking the queen. Slocum knew it would be only a flip or two more of the cards and the professor would lose one of the doubled and redoubled bets.

Slocum smiled slightly when the young woman with the diminutive scholar looked away from the flying cards and caught his eye. He knew he ought to let the con game continue. Life on a train was difficult at the best of times and many of the confidence men would see little for their efforts, other than getting booted off by Union Pacific conductors. But the woman stared at him, her gaze dropping demurely for a moment, then locking again with a boldness Slocum found enchanting.

He gestured to her to join him. She stiffened slightly and

shook her head the barest amount. Slocum silently mouthed "Please" and she cast a quick look at her companion. He was lost in the movement of the three cards, under and over, back and forth, the bet reaching a dollar now. Coming to a quick decision, she stood and made her way back along the aisle of the rattling car to stand before Slocum.

He looked up at her and found her taller than he had thought—and much lovelier.

"I don't mean to be forward, ma'am," Slocum said, touching the brim of his Stetson, "but the man with your husband is a crook. He's a cheat and—"

"I beg your pardon," she said. "My husband?"

"The gentleman you were sitting with. The one being cheated by the cardsharp. Three card monte is a sleight of hand game. It's not fair."

"You mean Professor Malloy," she said, laughing. Slocum thought silver bells rang. He had to shake himself to be sure it was only the young lady's laughter. "We are not married, sir. Oh, it is quite proper, the professor and I. You see, I am his assistant."

"I'm sure," Slocum said, "you do not want to see him lose money to chicanery. When the bet gets large enough, he'll never find the queen. The gambler will have palmed it and replaced it with another card."

"But the queen is marked," the woman said, eyes wide and innocent.

"That's the trick," Slocum said. "Excuse me. My name is John Slocum. Please sit down for a moment, and I'll explain."

"Thank you, Mr. Slocum. My name is Polly Greene."

"Miss Greene, the gambler wants your companion to think he can always pick out the card. It's part of the trick. Another card marked in the same way will be substituted. It's not hard, if you have nimble fingers and a little greed on your side."

"Greed? Why do you say that, Mr. Slocum?"

"The mark—your friend—will be watching the coins bet slide over the board. A quick movement replaces the queen. None of the cards chosen then will be right, and he will lose."

"I am sure Professor Malloy could afford to lose a dollar or two," Polly Greene said. "He is very wealthy. But more than this, he can watch out for himself, even against such a rogue. He is a clever man—some say brilliant."

Slocum fought to keep from staring at her. In spite of the rigors of railroad travel, Polly appeared fresh. She blushed fetchingly when it became apparent how Slocum studied her so closely.

"I apologize," Slocum said quickly. "It is not often a woman so beautiful travels on this train."

"You come this way often, Mr. Slocum?" Her flush went away and again she boldly stared back at him.

"No," Slocum said, "but I find myself wondering why you are traveling toward the Great Salt Lake with the professor."

She laughed her magical laugh again and Slocum was enchanted. "The professor is a paleontologist, a noted lecturer at Harvard University in Cambridge. I work as his assistant and one day hope to achieve his degree of knowledge. He is quite a remarkable soul, Professor Hercules Malloy."

Slocum kept from smirking. Hercules? The natty little man being cozened out of his money?

"You must think I am unlearned, but I don't rightly know what a paleontologist is," Slocum admitted. He would have admitted that he was responsible for the War Between the States, shot Lincoln, and had gone to the moon to keep Polly seated across from him and talking for even a minute longer. A faint whiff of her perfume caught on the hot breeze blowing through the window and made the sweltering interior of the passenger car almost bearable.

"That is all right, Mr. Slocum. Not many do. It is a new field, one fraught with controversy. We study life from past geological periods. That is, we look for fossilized bones and try to determine what manner of beast left them behind. Some of the bones are exceptionally old, many thousands of years old, though that is a point of debate, also."

"You're looking for old bones?" Slocum thought of all the cow skulls he had seen in his days riding herd up the Goodnight-Loving Trail, and the bleached bones of predators and prey—and humans. Polly Greene hardly seemed the type to root about in the dirt, hunting such debris. Rather, he pictured her at high tea in the Palace Hotel in San Francisco, the belle of society, the lady at the ball whom the men pursued and the women loathed.

"Something more exciting than that," she said, leaning forward in the seat. Slocum found himself bending closer to her, too, until their heads almost touched. Polly spoke in a soft, conspiratorial whisper almost drowned out by the clatter of steel wheels on uneven rails. "We are going to Bear Lake seeking a living monster, a survivor of a much earlier time."

"A monster?" This time Slocum found it impossible not to make light of her. "Why not look in the Great Salt Lake? It would leave a white track when it left the lake."

"Mr. Slocum, this is a serious matter, one reported by reputable sources. Why, the August 3, 1868, article by Mr. Joseph Rich in the *Deseret News* told of an unidentified beast observed swimming in Bear Lake. It defies categorization. We simply *must* find it and identify its genus and species."

She spoke so sincerely, Slocum didn't have the heart to ridicule her. In the desert, in the mountains, on the plains, men without food or water or companionship saw things that weren't there. Call them mirages or hallucinations, it didn't matter. Lonely, desperate, starving men believed what they saw, only to recant later after due consideration and a hearty good meal in the company of others.

"Of course, if possible, we would like to capture a specimen and return with it for the Harvard Museum." Polly saw nothing outrageous in crossing half the continent in search of a monster, hoping to net it and drag it back to Massachusetts.

"That's a mighty tall order," Slocum said. He started to draw her out more about her travels with Professor Malloy, but a man coming into the car caught Slocum's eye. He straightened in the seat and his hand involuntarily went to his six-shooter.

"Excuse me, Miss Greene," he said. "I see an acquaintance of mine. Got to catch up on old times." Slocum stood and made his way the length of the car, passing the professor and the three card monte dealer. Five dollars lay on the cardboard table, and the dealer's dexterous fingers flashed as the cards dropped. If he didn't skin the professor this time, he would the next.

But Slocum wasn't interested any longer in Professor Hercules Malloy or his card-playing friend. The man standing just inside the door, bending over a broken seat and trying to get it into place, held his complete attention. As he walked down the aisle of the swaying car, Slocum slid the leather thong from his six-shooter's hammer.

"Hello, Haskell," Slocum said. As the man looked up, startled, Slocum drew his pistol and swung it in a short arc, ending on the swarthy man's temple. A dull crunch was drowned out by the clatter of the wheels. Joe Haskell fell heavily, stumbling as he tried to step over the broken seat.

Slocum lowered his six-shooter and reached out with his left hand. The man's grimy collar provided a good enough grip for Slocum to push Haskell toward the open window. The man's head stuck out as Slocum lowered himself into the good seat facing the broken one.

"Wha—" Haskell struggled as the hot air cut at his face and hot cinders thrown back from the engine burned his skin.

Jerking harder, he tried to duck back into the car. Slocum rammed the barrel of his six-gun up into the man's gut.

"Be quiet, Haskell. Nobody'd hear the shot if I decided to pull the trigger. But then, what do I care if anyone hears? You owe me big."

"Slocum!" Joe Haskell thrashed about, arms flailing. Slocum backed off a mite, letting the man slip into the car. Haskell sank down, then tumbled even lower when the seat under him broke all the way. The man might as well have been stuffed into a basket for all the freedom of movement he had. And Slocum preferred it that way. He knew Haskell for the snake he was.

"Never expected to see me again, did you? You shot at my back and thought I was dead."

"I never, I mean, I—"

"You missed," Slocum said coldly. "And you owe me fifty dollars. You can welsh on your debts with others. Not with me."

"Slocum, it wasn't like that. Not at all. I reckoned you had upped and left Ellsworth."

It had been in Kansas, a year ago, after a long trail drive. The two had never been friends, and Haskell's poor betting in a game of high-low had made friendship out of the question. After losing, Haskell had run around like a wounded badger in a salt mine, moaning and bitching and snapping at everyone. But he had lost the money fair and square. He was too poor a gambler for Slocum to resort to cheating.

"You thought that because you tried to back-shoot me." Slocum cocked his six-gun, taking scant pleasure from the way Haskell's dark face drained of all color.

"I got the money. I'll pay up."

"Where you heading?" Slocum asked.

"Corinne."

"Why?" Slocum saw the hardness return to Haskell's face. The jaw firmed and the eyes turned cold. He knew

Slocum wasn't likely to plug him now. If the anger hadn't burned itself out, Joe Haskell would have been dead in a pool of his own blood.

"Ain't none of your business. And I don't know why I should pay you anything. I—"

Slocum twisted in the seat and jabbed out with his Colt. The muzzle dug into Haskell's ribs, making him groan in pain.

"All right, all right, you son of a bitch. I got the money. In my shirt pocket."

Slocum reached over and wiggled his fingers into the pocket matted with sweat against Haskell's chest. A thin wad of greenbacks rode there. He pulled them out. A quick count showed only forty dollars.

"You're ten short."

"So, I'll owe you, you—" Haskell grunted when Slocum poked him hard with the gun again.

"Maybe I'll just take it out of your worthless hide," Slocum said. He stood and moved away, his Colt Navy returning smoothly to its holster. "You still owe me ten."

"Go to hell, Slocum." Haskell struggled to get out of the broken seat. Slocum backed off and watched until Haskell fought his way free. For a moment, the burly man considered going for the six-shooter at his hip. When Joe Haskell saw the set to Slocum's chin and how ready he was for a fight, Haskell backed down quickly. Grumbling to himself, he fled the car, returning to the one from which he had come.

Slocum relaxed a little and shook his head. Joe Haskell was the last person he expected to see on the train. Haskell was an ornery varmint and no good. Slocum knew he'd have to watch his back until he was certain Haskell was either dead or far away again. Tucking the forty dollars into his own pocket, Slocum turned in the aisle to find another ruckus brewing.

The professor sat with a sizable wad of greenbacks in his

hand, mumbling to himself as he counted the bills one by one. He seemed oblivious to anything else happening around him.

''You can't do that to me,'' the gambler said, gritting his teeth. The three card monte dealer's face clouded with anger and his hand moved to the handle of a knife hidden up his sleeve. With a practiced gesture, he drew the slender, wicked blade and held it low and out of sight of the other passengers.

Professor Malloy was only an instant away from getting six inches of cold steel rammed into his belly.

2

Slocum moved like greased lightning. He could draw and fire before the gambler drove the tip of the shining knife into Professor Malloy's gut, but the report would draw unwanted attention. Slocum was on the run from men who wanted his scalp back in Cheyenne, and Joe Haskell would return like a bad penny and blame anything and everything on Slocum, no matter that the fight was between the professor and a shady gambler.

Two quick steps brought him level with the gambler. Turning, Slocum drove his elbow into the man's face. As the knife came up in a reflex motion, Slocum snared the gambler's wrist and twisted savagely. Bones broke as the knife dropped from the cardsharp's grip.

"You busted my hand," shrieked the gambler. "How the hell am I supposed to deal with a busted hand?"

A few others in the car, startled by the sudden outcry, stirred from their sluggish rest. Seeing nothing threatening to them, they turned away and tried to recapture the oblivion of dreamless sleep.

Slocum knelt and twisted the wrist in the other direction. More bones snapped. The gambler's face turned white with pain.

"Mr. Slocum, really," chided Polly Greene. She hurried down the aisle from where Slocum had been seated. It surprised him that the lovely blond had not returned to her own seat when he had left her so abruptly. It also pleased him that she had waited for him to come back. "You have no—"

"You are hurting him," Professor Malloy said. "Let him be."

Slocum didn't release his grip. He leaned over the gambler and picked up the knife and showed it to both the professor and his pretty assistant. Polly said something Slocum didn't catch. All Malloy said was, "My goodness."

Heaving, Slocum pulled the gambler to his feet and dragged him along behind. Fumbling, Slocum opened the door leading onto the platform between cars. With a heave, Slocum brought the monte dealer around and shoved him off the train. The man cried out once before he hit the hard desert and started rolling down the incline into a dry arroyo. Slocum went back to the professor's seat. He picked up the cardboard tray and four cards, and he tossed those out the window. Looking around, Slocum saw he had rid the train of the gambler with a minimum of fuss. Hardly any of the passengers, other than Polly Greene and her employer, had noticed the scuffle. That suited Slocum just fine.

"He was cheating you," Slocum accused.

"Oh, yes, I know, I know," said the professor. "How else do you think I won all his money?" Malloy held out the wad of greenbacks. "When he substituted the fourth card for the queen, I merely told him I could win by logical deduction. After all, I am a university professor."

"I don't understand." Slocum stared at the money in the dapper man's hand.

"I picked one card, then quickly turned over the other two. By deduction, if neither card I turned over was the queen, the remaining one had to be. Of course, it wasn't, since he had replaced it. But my logic was infallible." The professor sat quietly, counting the money he had won. Slocum wondered if the man would wear the ink off the bills counting and recounting.

"You handled yourself well, Mr. Slocum," complimented Polly Greene. "You are no stranger to perilous situations."

"I get by," Slocum said.

"Thank you for your timely intervention. I had not considered the possibility that he might try to harm me. I never saw the knife until you showed it to me," the professor said. Peering at Slocum over the tops of his spectacles, the man seemed to be judging him. Slocum didn't much care for that.

"If you'll excuse me—"

"One moment, sir," spoke up Malloy. "Since Miss Greene has spent some time at the rear of the car talking to you, I must assume you know of our expedition."

"To find a monster swimming around in Bear Lake," Slocum said, trying to keep his voice neutral. He didn't want to show too much scorn for their trip. He had been raised to respect his elders, and Polly was a very pretty woman. It never paid to insult a pretty woman.

"Yes, something on that order," Professor Malloy said, as if lecturing a class. "Now, you see how inept we are in dealing with the local ruffians. Perhaps I can persuade you to—I believe the term is *hire on*—as our guide—or perhaps the correct word is *scout*. At any rate, we need your assistance to be sure we aren't set upon by ruffians such as that gambler." Malloy extended the roll of greenbacks he had taken from the three card monte player.

Slocum blinked in surprise. He had forty dollars from Haskell riding high in his pocket. With the winnings from the Cheyenne poker game, he was richer than he had been in years. A few dollars more to go on a wild-goose chase didn't interest him.

"Much obliged, but I don't think so."

Slocum saw the professor look at Polly, who nodded quickly. They worked together well as a team.

"This is to be considered a down payment, five hundred dollars to follow. That is in addition, of course, to expenses."

"Five hundred?" For a moment, Slocum couldn't believe the princely sum the professor rattled off so easily. He turned to Polly, who smiled winningly. She nodded slowly. That, as much as the money, convinced Slocum. He wasn't heading to anywhere as much as he was going from.

"We will disembark at Corinne, head north to the Utah-Idaho border as if we were traveling to Soda Springs, but we will not go that far."

"The trail's not too hard," Slocum said, considering the professor's request. "I don't know the country all that well, but Frémont explored all around there. Maps will be easy to come by. It'll be like we're heading up to the Oregon Trail."

"See, professor? He does know the area. I told you!" Polly's face glowed with achievement.

Slocum frowned as he wondered when she had told Malloy this.

"I saw you earlier, Mr. Slocum, when you were dusting off your hat. I said to Professor Malloy that you had the appearance of a trailsman, a true scout of the West." Polly's face flushed again, and Slocum wondered what thoughts raced through her head. She nervously tucked more blond hair under her stylish hat, then pushed past him to sit beside the professor. As Polly moved past, her firm breasts rubbed across Slocum's arm in what he took to be an invitation.

"I'll do everything I can," Slocum said, staring at her.

"I'm sure you will, Mr. Slocum," said Professor Malloy, eagerly looking around the car. "I wonder if there are any more three card monte dealers here?"

"Corinne's only a few miles down the line from Promontory Summit," Slocum said, helping Polly from the railroad car.

Professor Malloy jumped down lightly beside her and looked around, as if expecting to see his monster lurking on the small loading platform.

"Miss Greene is perfectly aware of the geography, Mr. Slocum," Malloy said briskly. "You need not lecture her. She is an apt pupil and very well-educated. That is why I selected her from all my students to make this trip."

Slocum kept from laughing at the small scholar. He didn't doubt Polly Greene was capable; he simply didn't believe this was the professor's only reason for bringing her halfway across the country. She was pretty as a picture and had to be a danged sight better to travel with than most any other student.

"I think Mr. Slocum was hinting at something else, professor," Polly said. She clung to Slocum's arm as if he might bolt and run off. "What is it, sir? Please. Be direct."

"Very well. Corinne's a railroad town. That means most of it was built because the Union Pacific came through. There's not much more than saloons, dance halls, and horny men here. When the construction on the railroad died down, most of the population moved on. There's not much besides supplying the Union Pacific that keeps anyone here."

"You're saying it is a rough-and-tumble city?" Polly squeezed even tighter on his arm. He wondered if she had seen any city rougher than Boston.

"Reckon I am," Slocum allowed. "Last I heard, there're two dance halls, thirteen saloons, and more than eighty soiled doves who service the railroad crews."

"Cyprians? My," Polly said, daintily touching her lips with her hand. Slocum began to have doubts about the trip to Bear Lake. The country wasn't as rugged as some he knew of in the Wasatch Mountains, but even with a good road and fair weather, these two were out of their element. He'd have to nursemaid them both.

"See to our provisions, sir," ordered Professor Malloy.

"Here is enough to get a start on the supplies."

Slocum took the thick roll of bills and quickly stuffed it into the front of his shirt. He didn't bother counting it. Several hundred dollars was enough to get any man in Corinne het up enough to kill.

"A word of advice, professor. Don't go flashing around money like that. These aren't the richest men in the world, but they just might be the toughest."

"I understand, Mr. Slocum. I grew up in New York City and am acquainted with lawlessness. Miss Greene and I shall find a diner and wait for you."

"Go on and eat your fill," Slocum said. As much as he'd like to break bread with Polly Greene, he doubted his table manners were much good after so many months on the trail and in frontier towns. "I'll grab some chuck later."

"As you wish. Come along, my dear. I am famished." Professor Malloy held out his arm and Polly took it. Together, they strolled off into Corinne, hunting for a place to eat. Slocum hung back for a spell, watching to be sure they found a decent place and got inside without being molested. Although it was only a little past two in the afternoon, the saloons were already filling with thirsty men hunting for diversion—any diversion. Hurrahing a college professor and his pretty assistant would be just the thing to take the edge off boredom.

Satisfied that Polly and the professor were safe for the time being, Slocum set off to find a mercantile with supplies enough to keep them in feed and gear for a week. Corinne had only one general store, and Slocum spent the better part of an hour dickering with the owner over the blankets, victuals, and other goods they would need.

Leaving the store, Slocum looked around for a livery. He needed no fewer than three horses and a sturdy buckboard for packing their supplies. As he started down the street, he passed in front of the assay office. A huge man bumped into him, almost knocking him from his feet.

"Why, li'l feller, I didn't see you. Lemme hep you up."
A hand twice the size of Slocum's reached down and
grabbed his arm. Immense strength flowed as the hard rock
miner pulled Slocum back to his feet. "I surely am sorry,
but I'm so danged happy, I wasn't lookin' where I was
goin'."

"So offer to buy the man a drink, Tork," piped up a
second miner, shorter and even stockier than his partner.
"It's the least we can do."

"I could do with some whiskey," Slocum said, eyeing the
men. "What makes you in such an all-fired hurry?"

"We done struck it big," crowed the giant who had
knocked Slocum over. "My name's Tork Beckwourth, and
I'm rich!"

"And I'm his partner." The other man thrust out a grimy
paw. Slocum shook.

"His name's Gold Tooth Lawton, as if you couldn't tell."
Tork Beckwourth grabbed his partner's head and pulled his
jaws wide open. The front tooth shone brightly in the
afternoon Utah sunlight. "He had that put in with the very
first nugget we pulled from our mine. Now he kin have his
whole danged head done, if'n it suits him."

"Might just do that. Come along, stranger," Lawton said,
guiding Slocum toward the nearest saloon. "Here, lookee
here. See this? It's from a new vein we uncovered."

Gold Tooth Lawton thrust a huge chunk of rock in Slocum's direction. Slocum had worked gold mines in his day
and knew something of assaying. He held the rock out in the
sun and saw how the light played off the thick vein running
through the rock. He let out a low whistle.

"This is worth a young fortune," he said. "It must assay
out at five ounces to the ton."

"A man what knows his ore," Beckwourth crowed. "We
worked that worthless hell pit for more 'n two years and it

finally spat out something worthwhile.''

''Yep, that's the truth. The mine's out near Bear Lake,'' Lawton said.

Slocum drew away slightly as they entered the saloon and Beckwourth called out, ''Drinks for everybody!''

The roar that rose convinced Slocum the two miners weren't looking to keep their claim secret. He let the rush of miners push him toward one end of the bar. He got his shot of whiskey and was content to watch the frantic press of men. Slocum listened to the telling and retelling of how the two miners had finally struck it rich until he got tired. He ordered a drink of his own, used one of Professor Malloy's greenbacks to pay for it, and gnawed on pig's knuckles and pickles shoved toward him by the barkeep.

When he got tired of the crowd, Slocum made his way to the doors. He turned and saw Tork Beckwourth standing on a table at the rear of the saloon, showing in great detail how he had unearthed the rich vein of gold in his mine. Slocum shook his head. Sudden wealth made every man the center of attention. He pushed through the swinging doors and went back into the street to hunt down a livery stable and get the horses and buckboard.

Slocum froze when he saw Gold Tooth Lawton two doors down, in front of the general store. The miner spoke earnestly to Joe Haskell. From the way they stood almost face to face, the men knew one another and this was no chance meeting. The miner never once flashed his gold nugget as he had done with everyone he had encountered since leaving the assay office, and Haskell kept pointing north out of town while Lawton shook his head. Finally, the pair walked away together, going toward the railroad depot. Neither had spotted Slocum.

Torn between finding out what business Haskell had with the lucky miner and tending to his own business, Slocum finally decided it was none of his concern what Haskell and

Gold Tooth Lawton said to one another. Still, as he went about the purchase of three horses and a buckboard, he couldn't keep the men out of his mind. Haskell was a sidewinder, never coiled but always ready to strike dangerously. But Haskell had seemed to listen more than talk to the hard rock miner.

Shaking his head, Slocum went to find the professor and Polly Greene. They sat outside the café, talking with a grizzled old prospector who regaled them with tall tales of monsters and Indian ghosts.

"Mr. Slocum," greeted Polly. "This gentleman was telling us about the monster in the lake. It is common knowledge here!"

"If I know these folks," Slocum said, eyeing the old galoot picking his broken black teeth with the tip of a knife, "they'd be out there hunting for it—with an eye toward steaks on the dinner table."

"Might be," the old geezer said. "Might be some folks what done that very thing never came back."

"We shall see for ourselves," Professor Malloy said briskly. "Thank you for your time." He thrust out his hand. The old man stared at it for a second, then smiled his broken-toothed smile and shook.

"A real pleasure talkin' with you, perfesser." The man leaned back in his chair and set to carving on a piece of yellow pine.

As Polly, Hercules Malloy, and Slocum crossed the street heading for what Slocum thought to be the only decent hotel in Corinne, the scholar said, "Tripe."

"Beg pardon?" Slocum turned and stared at the short man.

Malloy took off his spectacles and polished them with a silk handkerchief. "Bunk. Tripe. Nothing but fable. He knew nothing of the Bear Lake denizen."

"I'm glad you think that. There's more hot air being

vented around a town like this than you might expect.''

"He thought me nothing but a gullible easterner. I read it plainly on his face."

"Don't think too badly of him. Life gets dull in a place like this." Slocum had been in town only an hour and already he wanted to leave. "I have the supplies and can get you put up in the hotel."

"Very well," Professor Malloy said, looking up at the two-story structure, as if judging if it might collapse if he set foot on the top floor. "I want to advise you fully about the creature we seek in Bear Lake. I believe Miss Greene has mentioned Joseph Rich's article. From this we can deduce—"

"That's all right, professor. We'll have plenty of time in the morning, when we get on the road for the lake."

Professor Malloy walked off, muttering about the monster. Polly shot Slocum a smile and hesitated, as if deciding whether to accompany him or her employer. Malloy won out. She cast one final glance over her shoulder, then entered the hotel with the professor.

Slocum had done his duty. His belly grumbled a mite. The small bit of food had settled and demanded company, so Slocum decided to choose another saloon, and he walked down the middle of the street, hunting for a good one. He entered Ben's Drink Emporium and found it to his liking. A huge picture of a nude woman hung over the bar and a faro game proceeded slowly at the rear of the large main room. Slocum went to the bar and ordered whiskey.

Barely had he lifted the shot glass to his lips when he overheard the conversation between two men down the bar.

"I seen it, I tell you. As big as life. Bigger!"

"You had a snootful of whiskey, that's your problem," complained the other.

"No, sir, I didn't. I needed a shot when I seen it! A monster, and there it was swimmin' around smack dab in the middle of Bear Lake!''

Slocum expected the second man to launch a scathing verbal assault. Instead, he shook his head slowly and replied, ''Parson Hurwell said he saw something out there, too. Can't believe it—just can't, but the parson's a truthful man.'' He knocked back his drink, stared at his companion, and added, ''Never heard you tell much of a lie, either.''

Slocum started to speak to the men, then clamped his mouth shut. Maybe the professor was onto something important, after all.

3

"Barkeep," called Slocum, motioning the man over. The portly bartender put down a dirty rag he had used to mop up spills on the bar and waddled over, twirling one side of his waxed mustache back into shape.

"Another?"

"Do it," Slocum said, watching more amber liquor slosh into his glass. "What do you know about those two down the bar?"

"Who? Them?" The barkeep tipped the whiskey bottle in the direction of the pair just finishing their drinks. The pair left the saloon, muttering between themselves. "That there's Elias Kenyon and Ash Wallings. Don't rightly know what they do for a living, but they always seem to have enough money to pay for their drinks and gamble a little. From their look and how dusty they always are, they must be miners."

"What kind of men are they?"

"Kind? No better or worse than any other around here." The barkeep stepped back and stared at Slocum. "I'd say, no better than you."

"And no worse," Slocum finished for him, smiling wryly. He knew when he heard a man not wanting to answer a question directly. "What I meant, are they more likely to spend time with Parson Hurwell or some whore?''

''Depends on whether it's Sunday. Can't see either Kenyon or Wallings passing up the chance to spend fifty cents on a girl, but the parson'd be able to call 'em by name if he saw 'em. He knows purty near everybody in these parts.''

Slocum knew he wasn't getting anywhere. The barkeep kept edging around a direct answer.

''What of the monster out there in the lake?''

The barkeep shrugged. ''Never seen it myself, but enough have. That why you're askin' after Wallings and Kenyon? They both been claimin' to see it out near the lake.''

This was the first solid fact Slocum had gotten from the barkeep. And from the way the man worked on his stringy mustache, it was likely to be the last.

''Much obliged,'' Slocum said, polishing off his drink. He decided to saunter over to the hotel and tell the professor what he had heard. The hunt for monsters might not be the foolish waste of time and money Slocum had thought at first.

As he stepped into the street, squinting in the bright sunlight, he heard angry voices coming from the alley beside the saloon. Ben's Drink Emporium hadn't been built too solidly, and the frame leaned toward the alley. When a heavy body slammed into the side of the building, shingles rained down from the roof and the wall sagged even more. Slocum walked to the end of the boardwalk and looked down the alley.

His hand whipped toward his Colt Navy. He checked the move, more curious than anxious to fill Joe Haskell with bullets. For the third time that day, he had come across Haskell.

Haskell shoved Ash Wallings hard against the wall. Before the miner could recover, Haskell pushed him again. Wallings's partner, Elias Kenyon, protested. Haskell swung about, his six-shooter slipping from its holster. He buffaloed the miner, driving him to his knees.

Slocum didn't see six-guns at the hips of either miner. They carried knives sheathed at their belts, and maybe one in their boot tops, but Haskell gave them no chance to use their weapons.

"Touch those toad stickers and you'll be pushin' up daisies." Haskell took another step back and covered the two men. Kenyon rubbed the side of his head where Haskell had laid the gun barrel and Wallings bared his teeth in a silent snarl.

"I'll rip your head off," Wallings threatened. He subsided when Haskell cocked his six-shooter and pointed it squarely at the miner.

"You might try," Haskell snapped. "You won't get close enough to finish the job. Now, you boys listen up. I don't cotton to you owlhoots spreadin' lies."

"They ain't lies!" protested Kenyon. "We seen the monster. We have!"

"You so much as whisper that in public and I'll cut your tongues out and stuff them down your throats," the gunman said. "You don't know what you're gettin' into with those tall tales."

"Ain't no tall tale. Wallings has seen it. And I believe him. So's the parson. He seen it, too!"

Haskell moved fast. He stepped up, measured the distance, and kicked the fallen Kenyon in the belly. The miner folded like a bad poker hand, retching his guts out on the ground. Haskell spun quickly, his six-gun covering Ash Wallings.

"I ought to whale the tar out of the pair of you." Haskell went on to detail the bloody horrors he would visit on the men if they so much as mentioned a creature in Bear Lake again.

Slocum considered going to the miners' aid, then hesitated. He heard the argument raging down the alley and was confused by it. Why did Haskell want to stifle any mention of a monster swimming around in Bear Lake? For a man who had just arrived in Corinne, he got around fast and caused a powerful lot of disturbance.

Haskell kicked Kenyon again. The miner's partner dived onto Haskell, thick arms circling the gunman's shoulders. Haskell's pistol discharged, and Slocum knew he had to do something to stop the fight. Wallings and Kenyon had information Professor Malloy might find useful. If Haskell killed them, that knowledge would be gone forever.

He started down the alley, then stopped when he saw a tall, hatchet-faced man hurrying across the street, making a beeline for the alley. The battered tin star shining on the man's vest told Slocum to back off. He had enough warrants following him around, and one might have landed on this lawman's desk.

The marshal pushed past Slocum without even noticing him.

"You hold on there," called the marshal, his hand going to his holstered pistol when he saw that Haskell had drawn his six-gun. "I don't want anyone gettin' hurt."

Haskell's six-shooter came up, and the man's finger curled again on the trigger. The bullet came singing in the marshal's direction, but Wallings dragged Haskell's arm down, causing the shot to go wild.

"He done shot me, marshal. He shot me, but I got him!" The burly miner swung a fist like the head of a sledgehammer and landed a heavy blow on Haskell's chin. The punch rocked the gunman but didn't stop him from fighting.

He clumsily swung his gun and landed a glancing blow on the side of Wallings's head, as he had already done to Elias Kenyon. The impact jarred Ash Wallings, but he kept fighting.

By this time, a small crowd had gathered at the mouth of the alley. The barkeep rushed from the saloon and grumbled, "It took the marshal long enough to get here. I sent a boy to fetch him ten minutes ago. Those fellers are gonna kill themselves if he don't do somethin' quick to stop 'em.''

Slocum knew this was a lie. The two miners and Joe Haskell hadn't been in the alley for more than five minutes, but he understood the barkeep's anxiety. Every time one or the other of the battling men hit the wall of the saloon, it leaned away a bit more. If the marshal didn't quell them soon, the whole structure might collapse.

"Drop that hogleg, damn you!" shouted the marshal. He struck Haskell's wrist with the side of his six-shooter. Haskell's grip on his gun weakened. This gave Ash Wallings the chance to wrestle it from him. Haskell kicked out and got to his feet, getting ready to turn rabbit and run.

"Take one step and I'll ventilate you," the marshal warned, his six-gun steady and centered on Haskell's chest. "I don't know who the hell you are, but you're spendin' time in my jail."

"Marshal," warned Slocum. "The miner with the gun."

The lawman turned his attention to Wallings. The miner picked up Haskell's gun and trained it on the marshal's prisoner.

The lawman knocked the gun away just as Wallings pulled the trigger. The third round from Haskell's six-shooter went into the dirt. This time, the marshal wrested it from Wallings and tucked it into his belt for safety.

"You got reason to cut him down, but you got to abide by the law. See to your partner," the marshal said curtly. Ash Wallings muttered under his breath, but he knelt and helped Kenyon sit up. The fallen miner had turned pasty white under his leathery complexion. Unable to speak, Elias Kenyon gobbled like a turkey, then puked again.

"You two get on out of town. I don't want to see your ugly faces again this week," the marshal told the miners.

"But, marshal, he was the one—" Wallings pointed at Haskell.

"I saw enough to know. Get on out of here. And you,

mister, you're coming with me.'' The lawman took Haskell's arm and shoved him out of the alley. Slocum stepped back and watched as the marshal herded a protesting Joe Haskell toward the Corinne jail. The building didn't look like much, but Slocum had been inside enough Utah jails to know the cells were tight enough to hold the likes of Haskell.

He considered going over to talk with the lawman and try to find out what Haskell's interest was in keeping the miners silent about what they had seen. He shook off the notion. The law in Utah kept wanted posters longer than in most places, partly because the Mormon population didn't have as many outlaws—not unless you counted having more than one wife as a crime.

Slocum knew the poster he feared the most went back to his days after the war. He had been on the mend from getting gutshot when he got home to Calhoun, Georgia. A carpet-bagger judge had taken a fancy to Slocum's Stand, property that had been in the Slocum family for generations, since King George I had deeded it over. No taxes had been paid on the land, claimed the judge.

The judge and a hired gun had ridden out to confiscate the farm. Slocum knew better than to fight with words. No Reconstruction court would side with a former Confederate officer, especially one who had ridden with Quantrill. Slocum didn't argue. He just used the six-shooters he had brought home from the war. Then John Slocum had ridden off, never looking back.

The crime of judge killing had dogged his steps ever since, and he wasn't going to place bets on whether the lawman in Corinne, Utah, had one sitting in his file cabinet.

Slocum went to talk with Wallings and Kenyon, but the men had already gone. Slocum wandered around a while, hunting for them, but they had taken the marshal's words at face value and hightailed it. After the punishment Kenyon had received from Haskell, Slocum didn't much blame them.

And in spite of Wallings's claim that Haskell had shot him, Slocum didn't think the miner moved as if he had a slug buried in him anywhere.

Steps turning back to the hotel, Slocum decided it was time to tell Professor Malloy what he had found out. There might not be a monster in the lake, but the way folks talked about it, taking a good look wasn't going to be a waste of time.

Slocum went into the hotel. The room clerk looked up.

"Afternoon, Mr. Slocum," he greeted. "You wantin' your room key?"

"Reckon so," Slocum said. He had little enough in the way of gear. There hadn't been time in Cheyenne to collect all his belongings. "I need to talk with Professor Malloy. Is he in his room?"

" 'Fraid not. He left well nigh fifteen minutes ago. He was carryin' a fancy carved walking stick, as if he intended to do some explorin' on foot."

"Let me have my key anyway," Slocum said. He could use some rest. Starting up the stairs, he was aware of eyes on him. At the top of the stairs, he stopped and looked along the narrow corridor. One door stood slightly ajar and a large gray eye peered out at him. Slocum tipped his hat in that direction and said, "Afternoon, Miss Greene."

The door opened, and a flustered Polly Greene called to him.

"Come in, Mr. Slocum. I didn't mean to spy. I heard footsteps and thought it might be Professor Malloy returning."

"The clerk said he went on a hike. Were you expecting him back so soon?"

Slocum saw past the woman to where she had pulled up a chair by the window. She must have seen him crossing the street, if she had been sitting there—and Polly had to know it wasn't her employer who had returned.

"Do you think it is proper for me to come in?" Slocum asked. He didn't want to besmirch her reputation.

She reached out and grabbed his arm, dragging him inside. He entered, curious at her behavior. Taking off his hat, he held it and waited for her to tell why she needed to talk to him so badly.

Polly closed the door and leaned against it. "I saw what happened across the street. Are you hurt?"

"Hurt? Me? No. Why'd you think that?"

"I heard gunfire, then the marshal came out of the alley with that ruffian from the train. The one with whom you had argued."

"Nothing to fret over much, Miss Greene. That was just an old misunderstanding. It's all taken care of now. But I did want to talk to the professor about something I overheard before the fight in the alley."

"Call me Polly," she said, coming closer. Slocum saw the devil dancing in the woman's pale eyes. Her fingers stroked over his stubbled beard, then moved lower to sneak inside his shirt front. He felt her fingertips against his chest. Then she moved even lower.

Slocum caught her wrist. "Do you know what you're doing?" he asked.

"Wait and see," she said. Her tongue came out and licked her lips, just a little, then she surged forward and kissed Slocum hard. He didn't waste any time responding to the kiss. He might have seen a more beautiful woman somewhere, but he couldn't remember when or where. And he wasn't going to pass up what she so willingly offered to him.

Polly broke off the kiss and stepped back half a pace. Her breasts rose and fell heavily. She chewed on her lower lip as she stared into Slocum's green eyes.

"That set my heart to pounding, John. How about yours?"

"More 'n that is throbbing," Slocum admitted. He grunted

when Polly unfastened his gun belt and tossed it aside, then began kneading the thick mound growing at his crotch.

"You're right," she said. Her nimble fingers danced here and there, working on the buttons holding him inside. Slocum stroked over her silken blond hair, then held her firmly for a moment.

"What would the professor say if he found us together?"

"He won't. Besides, he's my instructor, not my father. I learn from him, and I get paid a decent stipend for my assistance. The obligation I have to him ends there."

Slocum found himself speechless. She slithered her hands down and fumbled around inside his trousers, pulling out the hardening manhood hidden inside. He moaned softly when he felt her hot breath gusting around his aroused flesh, and he almost lost control when her ruby lips circled the tip of his manhood. Her tongue teased and tickled, stroked and stimulated. When Polly's head began moving back and forth so she could take more of him into her mouth, he had to stop her.

"That's almost more than I can stand. I want more. You're so damned lovely! I want more."

Polly laughed delightedly and stood slowly, shrugging her shoulders to get free of her blouse. She worked for a moment at her waist and then stepped from her skirt. Clad only in frilly undergarments, Polly Greene pressed hard against Slocum, pulling his face down to hers for another kiss.

Now it was Slocum's turn to give as well as receive. He found the ties and one by one undid them until the lacy underwear fell away, leaving the eager woman completely naked. Slocum's hands dipped down to cup her large breasts. His thumbs pressed into the hard nubbins of her nipples as he squeezed down. A tremor passed through her.

"Can't stand it. You take away my strength, John. Give me yours!" She reached out and gripped his length, pulling it toward her. Together they sagged onto the narrow bed.

Polly wiggled over and lay on her back, slender legs spread in an inviting V.

For a moment, Slocum was content simply to stare at her naked loveliness. Every bit of her trim body was perfect, milky white, satiny smooth. He moved between her legs and bent forward, kissing her fervently even as she tugged at him. He felt the tip of his fleshy stalk brush across the fleecy triangle between her thighs. Then he sank deeply into her moist interior.

He stopped as if trapped in amber. She surrounded him with her feminine flesh totally, captivating him. Heat and pressure mounted as her muscles tensed around him. Then Slocum pulled back slowly. A new shudder of delight passed through the woman's body. When only the thick head of his manhood remained within her nether lips, he took a moment to stare at her again.

"So beautiful," he whispered. She lay with her eyes closed, blond hair tossed back and to one side on the pillow. Her large breasts rose and fell as she breathed heavily. The nubs might have been coppery pennies, but no hard metal ever pulsed with lust as Polly did. Slocum bent and licked over one breast, then moved quickly to duplicate his efforts on the other. Through her nipples he felt her frenzied heart beating.

"Don't do this to me, John. Don't torment me. I want you, I want you all the way!" She reached out to pull at him. Slocum didn't need to be urged. The pressure in his loins had mounted steadily since the first brush of Polly's lips across his tip.

He entered her slowly and pulled back at the same speed. He tried to keep a gentle motion back and forth, but lust seared his veins and drove him to ever-increasing speed. Heat burned at his length. He felt her responding fully, her legs curling up and then circling his waist to make sure he didn't go anywhere.

Slocum would have been a fool to stop. He fell into the age-old rhythm of a man loving a woman and sent Polly Greene sailing on the wings of desire. Then the fire burning deep within him grew hotter. He began to boil and no longer controlled himself. Hips ramming hard, he tried to bury himself completely within her body.

Polly shrieked and moaned and clung to him as he spilled his seed.

Sweaty, exhausted, he sank down into the circle of her arms. She kissed him gently. He moved around a little so he could look into her face. If he had died and stared at an angel, he couldn't have been more content.

"For a schoolgirl, you surely do know how to . . ." Decency prevented Slocum from finishing.

Not so Polly Greene. "You're trying to say that I've learned my lessons? That I make love like a whore?"

"No!" Slocum was outraged at this. "No whore ever gave me the pleasure you just did."

"Well, it might have been an accident," Polly said lightly. "Are you interested in finding out?"

"What do you mean?"

They made love a second time, more slowly, with passion building more gradually—but Slocum had to allow the first time was no fluke. Nor was the third just before dawn the next day.

4

Slocum awoke when the first rays of dawn crept through the window in Polly's room. He pushed out of the bed without disturbing her. The sunlight shone off her blond hair, turning it into spun gold. He gathered his clothing and hurriedly dressed, worrying that Professor Malloy might have returned and heard them. They hadn't been too quiet about their lovemaking.

That had been fine with Slocum during the act. Now he worried about Polly's reputation.

He slipped from her room and went to his own across the hall, getting his gear laid out for the trip ahead of them. He had barely finished putting it on the bed when a sharp rap came at his door. He opened it to see Professor Hercules Malloy standing there.

For an instant, Slocum thought he had been caught and that the professor would fire him and send Polly packing back to Cambridge. Malloy pushed into the room and blustered around, waving his fancy carved walking stick.

"Everywhere in Corinne they talk of the monster," he said without preamble. "But I have found the single source most likely to be accurate and not mere fable. Are you ready to leave, Mr. Slocum? Time is of the essence. I can hardly wait to find this creature and write the paper about it. That will show them. It will show them all!''

"Your colleagues?'' Slocum asked, gathering the gear and slinging it over his shoulder.

"Who else?'' The dapper scholar stared up at Slocum, his eyes magnified by his spectacles. "I should not rush you, should I? It is so easy to forget others do not share my ideas of schedule and urgency.''

"Is Miss Greene ready?'' Slocum asked, knowing full well she was still in bed where he had left her only minutes earlier.

"She is a late riser. I thought to prepare everything for our journey before rousing her. She is the best student I ever had, in spite of her sedentary habits. Imagine. Sleeping until almost seven o'clock every day.'' The professor shook his head and clucked his tongue.

"Her habits seem just fine to me,'' Slocum said. The professor looked at him curiously, then turned and left the room without saying anything. Slocum settled his gear on his shoulder, stared at the still made bed, and realized he had wasted money. There hadn't been any need to rent this room for the night. But he hadn't known that when they checked in the afternoon before.

Slocum went into the hallway and saw the professor rapping at Polly's door.

"We leave in one hour, Miss Greene,'' the professor called. From inside the room came a mumbled reply. "Mr. Slocum is ready to go right now. Do not keep him waiting.'' Malloy peered at Slocum over the top of his spectacles, then bustled on down the stairs into the lobby. Slocum couldn't read the man's expression, but he thought it was one of suspicion.

Hesitating in front of Polly's door, Slocum considered ducking back in for a few minutes, but he held back. He knew the professor didn't want to be kept waiting for another half hour—and Slocum thought he and Polly would take longer than that.

Going downstairs, Slocum found the professor sitting cross-legged on the boardwalk in front of the hotel, talking with a young boy.

"You have seen it?" asked Professor Malloy.

"No, sir, I ain't, but my teacher has. Miz Smith was visitin' a sick kid up near the lake and she seen it. She *saw* it," the boy revised, looking around as if his teacher stood behind, waiting for poor grammar. "It was huge, she said. She told us about it in class."

"Your teacher is out at the schoolhouse?" Malloy asked.

"Well, no, sir. She's off visitin' other shut-ins. She has to do that about one week every other month. Some of her students can't get into Corinne all the time to go to school." The boy heaved a deep sigh. "Truth is, there ain't many of us here. Most of the town's owing to the Union Pacific and they don't bring wives or kids with them."

"Drifters," said Malloy, nervously rubbing the large knob at the end of his walking stick. "So you have no notion where your Miss Smith might be?"

"She'll be back come Monday next. Till then, we got a vacation."

"Vacation," snorted the professor. "I never had such a break in my schooling. Son, go home and get your school books. Study. Study hard."

"You goin' to hunt for the monster? Kin I go with you?"

"No, you may not. It might prove dangerous." Professor Malloy looked up and saw Slocum. "Mr. Slocum, please load the wagon. I have a few more people to talk with before we leave town."

"Straight to Bear Lake?" Slocum asked.

"Not quite. There are others I must speak with." The professor muttered to himself as he started walking. Slocum had seen drunks with a better sense of direction. Professor

Hercules Malloy had nothing but the monster on his mind. Slocum shook his head and started for the livery. He wasn't sure what to think about the monster. Strange things happened, but that didn't mean sea monsters existed.

And why would Joe Haskell threaten the two miners because they claimed they had seen it? Slocum couldn't make head nor tail of it.

"Hey, mister, you work for the professor?"

The towheaded boy trailed along behind him. Slocum nodded.

"I know everything about it. *Everything*," the boy insisted. "Take me along and I'll show you the exact spot where Miz Smith saw it."

"How'd she come to mention the monster?" Slocum asked, leading out the horses to hitch them to the buckboard. He finished with the team, then saddled his horse, a sturdy gray gelding that looked strong enough to ride day and night and still have enough left for another few yards.

"We was actin' up in class, and she tole us the monster would eat us all if we didn't behave." The boy shivered in recollection. "Don't know if she meant it, but it worked. We hushed right up."

"What did she say it looked like?"

The boy launched into an improbable description that grew as the telling stretched on. Slocum began to doubt the teacher had seen anything and had only spun the tale to keep her students in line. Like the others, more doubt existed after serious consideration than before.

So why was Haskell threatening Ash Wallings and Elias Kenyon if they told anyone of their encounter? Seeing a monster was harmless enough, on the face of it. Slocum thought the answer lay more with Joe Haskell than at the bottom of Bear Lake.

"Mr. Slocum!" came a voice he knew well. Slocum waited for Polly Greene to reach the buckboard before saying anything. He inclined his head slightly to indicate the boy, hoping she wouldn't say anything about how they had spent the night in front of him.

"I've got work to do," Slocum told the boy. "There's no place for you on this expedition."

"Who's she?"

"I'm Professor Malloy's assistant and student," Polly said.

"I've seen the monster!" the boy blurted. He chewed his lower lip and dropped his eyes to the ground, then sheepishly looked over at Slocum, as if begging him not to contradict him. Slocum understood. "I mean, I know someone who has. I can find the creature."

"Thank you for your offer," Polly said graciously, "but we have no idea how long we will be gone. I am sure your parents would worry if you were away long."

"Yeah, Ma would. Pa wouldn't like doing my chores, either."

"Run along," Slocum said. The boy reluctantly left, occasionally casting a furtive glance in Polly's direction. Slocum knew what thoughts ran through the boy's head. Monster or not, being on the trail with such a lovely woman was worth the time.

Slocum couldn't have agreed more.

"My trunk is on the walkway in front of the hotel. The clerk was kind enough to help me get it down."

"Let me help you up," Slocum said, enjoying the feel of his hands around the woman's trim waist as he helped Polly into the buckboard. The woman settled down, obviously not enjoying the hard, wooden seat. Slocum swung up and got the buckboard moving. His gray trailed along, its reins fastened to the rear.

"Last night was special, John," Polly said in a low voice. Her hand crept over and rested on his leg. For a moment, Polly was content with simply leaving it there but when she moved it higher on his thigh, then slid toward his crotch, Slocum got antsy.

"Not in public," he said. "Folks will talk."

"Let them," she said. "We will be gone from Corinne before noon. Who will care?"

"People talk, and the Mormon settlers in these parts are real sticklers for moral behavior."

Polly sniffed indignantly as she said, "They allow men to have several wives." In spite of this, the blond pulled her hand back by the time Slocum reined in by the pile of her belongings. The hotel clerk had added the professor's luggage to the stack.

"You travel light," Slocum observed, jumping down. He tossed the cases into the rear, then stopped when Polly laughed. "What'd I say?"

"The rest of the gear is still at the railroad depot. Professor Malloy has almost five hundred pounds of equipment. We shall need it to photograph the monster, when we find it, and there are other scientific instruments necessary for observation."

"Five hundred pounds?" Slocum scratched his head as he looked at the rear of the buckboard. He ought to have bought a freight wagon to haul that much equipment.

"Don't worry about it now, John. Professor Malloy will need only a few items at a time. It might prove necessary to return to Corinne and ferry it to our advance camp."

"Advance camp? You make this sound like a military campaign." Slocum climbed back into the box and squinted into the sun, hunting for the professor. The stylish scholar sat outside the saloon across the street, huddled with a grizzled old man who often spat into the street.

"He is forming a general picture of what residents think of the monster," Polly said, falling into a lecturer's style of speaking. "With proper background we can ascertain if—"

She broke off when Slocum snapped the reins to get the buckboard moving.

"Got to load the equipment," he told her.

"There's no need to be rude, John."

"Didn't mean to be. The more I hear about this monster, the less sure I am it exists. The only one I've come across who claims to see it isn't too believable." He remembered how Ash Wallings put away the whiskey and what his partner said about the sighting. Maybe Wallings had been liquored up and saw demons where none existed. Or maybe he simply enjoyed hearing his own voice. Men alone in the mines and on the farms scattered around Corinne hungered for human contact after being alone for long months. Any tale that drew a crowd fed their need for friendship.

"It must exist. There are too many reputable sightings for it to be a hoax," Polly said. "Mr. Rich is a reputable journalist. He would not make up the story for the sake of a byline."

"I've heard tell of more than one newsman writing up hoaxing stories as a joke. That Mark Twain fellow over in Nevada did a piece or two that was sky-high wild," Slocum said. He tucked the reins down at the foot of the buckboard box and hopped down. The stacks of equipment unloaded from yesterday's train rose up like a mountain to be climbed.

"Take only those crates marked with the numeral one," Polly said. "The railroad agent has guaranteed the safety of the rest while we are gone."

Slocum grunted as he began moving the bulky crates. It took some shifting and reloading, but he finally got the boxes into the rear of the buckboard, with room enough left for their supplies.

"Mr. Slocum, good, I see Miss Greene has supervised you properly. We must hurry if we are to find my last contact. I need only get his narrative. Here, Mr. Slocum, here is a map showing how to reach our informant's residence."

Slocum took the scrap of paper, turned it around and got his bearings. He tucked it into his shirt pocket, jumped up, and waited for the professor to crowd next to Polly. Slocum might have ridden the gray, but he didn't mind at all that Polly had to scoot over on the seat, her hip pressing into his.

As they drove from town, Slocum's thoughts meandered, going from his night with Polly to Professor Malloy's quest to find the Bear Lake monster and finally returning to the mystery of Joe Haskell's behavior. Slocum's old adversary had talked with the miner who had struck it rich—Gold Tooth Lawton—as if he had known him for some time, and then Haskell had gotten into a row with Ash Wallings and Elias Kenyon over their public accounts of sighting the monster.

None of it made much sense.

An hour down the road, Slocum saw a hovel alongside the trail. He pulled out the map Malloy had given him, and then frowned.

"Professor, somebody's been pulling your leg. That's the place where we're supposed to find your informant."

"Yes, yes, he is a Paiute scout. Quite reputable, from all I have learned in Corinne."

Slocum held his tongue. An Indian sat beside the ramshackle house, basking in the sun. At his feet were empty bottles. If Malloy got more than a string of snores for his effort, it would surprise Slocum. He fastened the reins, helped Polly down, and then walked behind the two researchers as they went to the sleeping Indian.

"Good day, sir," Malloy greeted. "I am investigating the creature residing in Bear Lake. Am I correct in assuming you are Dark Cloud?"

The Indian looked up, eyes bloodshot. A single movement of the head was all the answer Malloy received. It was enough for the professor. He dropped down beside the huddled Indian.

''Tell me what you've seen.'' Professor Malloy pulled out a small notebook and put a pencil to paper in anxious anticipation of all he would be told.

The Indian gasped, coughed, and spat a thick, black gob. Slocum had seen more than one Indian with consumption. He saw another one in Dark Cloud. With great deliberation, Dark Cloud began speaking.

Slocum drew Polly aside, though the woman was fascinated. ''See the whiskey bottles?'' He pointed to the empty bottles littering the ground. ''Anything Dark Cloud says isn't likely to mean much.''

''He was a scout for the cavalry,'' she said. ''He held responsible positions. There is no reason to disbelieve him.''

''He's likely to say anything to get a full bottle of rotgut,'' Slocum said in disgust. He walked away, fuming at the turn the search was taking. But as he walked, his thoughts turned back to the Paiute. The name Dark Cloud nudged his memory, though how, he was at a loss to say. When Professor Malloy called to him, Slocum walked back.

''Dark Cloud will accompany us to the lake. He knows where the monster enters and leaves. I can adequately control the team, if you care to ride your mount, Mr. Slocum.''

Slocum shrugged it off. He didn't mind riding next to Polly. Quite the contrary, but the professor obviously wanted to let Dark Cloud lead them to Bear Lake and the monster the Paiute claimed to have seen.

The team struggled and strained and got moving. Slocum rode alongside, occasionally glancing over at Dark Cloud. The man's hawklike profile again nudged his memory until Slocum had to speak up.

''Did you ride with Major Conroy's company?''

Dark Cloud turned and studied Slocum for a moment. He spat another black gob stained with blood, then nodded once.

''You kept him from being slaughtered, didn't you? I

heard the story a while back. You risked your life to keep him out of a Ute ambush.''

''I did that,'' Dark Cloud said. Even these few words caused him to start coughing. He reached under his blanket and pulled out a bottle of whiskey. He took half of it in a single draft, then shoved the cork back into the neck. ''Keeps the pain from growing too big,'' the Paiute explained.

Slocum knew others with consumption. He had crossed paths with Doc Holliday more than once. The Georgia gambler drank upwards of a quart of liquor a day, mostly to kill the pain. Dark Cloud's consumption ate him up inside. This changed Slocum's opinion of the Paiute—on one count. He still didn't believe Dark Cloud had seen any monster in Bear Lake and this was going to be wasted effort on their part.

Nearing sundown, they pulled off the deeply rutted road leading northward and cut over toward the lake. The sound of waves lapping against distant shores came to Slocum's ears before he caught the whiff of mountain lakes he remembered so well. Fish. The notion of pulling a few big-mouthed bass from the lake and frying them up for dinner turned a wild-goose chase into a worthwhile excursion.

''We must set up our equipment,'' Professor Malloy said to Polly. ''We will be at the shore soon. Dark Cloud says the creature enters and leaves at twilight. Definitely a crepuscular beast. I surmise that—''

Slocum rode on ahead, not wanting to listen to the technical discussion Malloy launched into. Polly seemed comfortable with the two-bit words. All Slocum wanted to do was get a glimpse of the lake and figure out where the best fishing might be.

He crested a rise and saw the lake stretched out before him. The shoreline curved about in a broad sweep, hiding a part of the lake from view. The shore was rocky and wouldn't take much in the way of tracks.

The smell of pine and fresh water on the wind made Slo-

cum take a deep breath. He wandered about, not really knowing what he sought—until times like this. The wind in the
pines, the lapping of water on the shore, the sight and sound
of small animals coming from their burrows for evening
feeding, the stark solitude all told him why he was alive.

The quiet was broken as Professor Malloy fought to get
the buckboard up the slope.

"Where is it, Dark Cloud?" asked the scholar, eager to
get on with his hunt. "Can you point out the spot?"

"Down there," said the Paiute scout. Dark Cloud pointed
at an angle across the small inlet toward the stony outjutting
into the lake.

"That's about the rockiest part of the lakefront," Slocum
said. "We ought to pitch camp, then go on foot." He eyed
the crates of equipment and worried what the professor might
want to take along. Luckily, Malloy's enthusiasm knew no
bounds. He had come too far to delay even a few minutes.

"We can leave our equipment. There's no one about. Let's
all go down. I want to see the spot where the creature goes
into the water. Lead the way, Dark Cloud."

The Indian wheezed and coughed, but kept up a decent
pace as they followed a game trail down the slope toward
the lake. Dark Cloud led, trailed closely by Professor Malloy.
Polly came next, and Slocum brought up the rear. Twenty
minutes of walking brought them to the edge of the lake.
Gentle waves came and went against the rock-strewn shore.

"That way. Out there. I go there to fish and saw it at
almost this time, but a week ago."

"Yes, yes, right away. We'll go right now."

"We might make better time if Dark Cloud remains here,"
suggested Polly. She fought to maintain the pace, her long
skirts getting in the way.

"You might want to stay with him, then," said Slocum.
He saw no reason for her to go traipsing along the shore,
maybe to turn her ankle on the large rocks.

"No! I am a scientist," she flared. Her passion died a mite as she added, "I am in training to be a scientist like Professor Malloy. I need to witness everything firsthand, if I am to be of any assistance to him."

"We can all go," Malloy said. "Dark Cloud must show me the precise spot. I need to sketch the tracks, study the terrain, take samples. Water, dirt, the very rocks! There is so much to do."

Darkness descended and Slocum found the going even harder. It took almost an hour to follow the curve of the shore out to the finger of land where Dark Cloud claimed to have found traces of the monster. As Slocum made his way along the rocky ground, he kept a sharp eye out for any sign of a large animal.

He saw nothing.

Disgusted, wet from the occasional slip into the lake, Slocum almost collided with Professor Malloy. The dapper scholar stood beside Dark Cloud. Polly quickly joined them.

"What have you found, professor?" she asked eagerly.

"There," Malloy said, hardly able to contain his excitement. "Dark Cloud says the creature's lair is in there!"

5

"Wait here while I take a look." Slocum pushed past Polly and the professor, almost slipped on the wet rocks, then got his footing. Carefully, Slocum made his way down a steep incline to a broad, rocky flat. To the right lay Bear Lake. To the left, where Dark Cloud had pointed, yawned a gaping dark hole large enough to drive a freight train into. Slocum touched the worn butt of his Colt Navy, then moved his hand away.

If he found anything fitting the dimensions of that hole, a six-shooter wouldn't be big enough. He wasn't certain a buffalo rifle would. Dropping to one knee, he ran his fingers over the damp rocks. He rubbed his fingers together, then sniffed at them. A pungent odor rose, making his nose wrinkle.

"What did you find, Mr. Slocum?" called the professor.

"Can't rightly say," Slocum answered. "There's spoor along here, but it's nothing I've ever seen before." He stood and walked back and forth across the broad area. A few dead fish lay far away from the edge of the lake, as if something had thrown them there, but he couldn't discount weather being responsible. A strong wind might blow the water up this far into the spit and leave a few desperate fish trapped on land to die and rot away.

"We want to come down. Is it safe?"

"Polly, wait, no, stay up there," Slocum said, aware that he had called her by her first name. Neither the professor, in his excitement, nor Dark Cloud in his silent contemplation of the lair, noticed. "I want to make sure it's safe."

"We are capable of dealing with the creature, Mr. Slocum. We're coming down." Professor Malloy began the tricky descent in the dark. Polly followed. Slocum couldn't tell if Dark Cloud joined them. He let out a gusty sigh. He found himself trying to imagine the size of the beast wallowing along this spit, going into the dark cavern ahead. All he could think was how huge it was.

He loosened his six-gun in his holster and headed into the mouth of the cave before the others could reach him. If there were any monster lurking in the cave, he wanted to flush it out. And if lead started flying, Slocum had to be certain Polly wasn't in the way.

His long stride carrying him across the rocks, he came to the mouth of the cave. A fetid odor hit him like a physical blow. Slocum had smelled similar aromas near coyote dens. He rubbed his nose and plunged on, the rim of the cave arching up over him and cutting off the last vestiges of light from the sky. He blundered along a few yards, then stopped to get his bearings.

The cave stretched deeper into the rocky peninsula, more than he would have thought, looking at it from outside. Behind him, Slocum heard Polly and the professor making their way toward him. And ahead? He could not tell.

"We need a torch," he called to them. "It's too dark to go any farther."

"We must, we must find out what's here," gasped Professor Malloy, sliding across the rocks in a hurry to find his monster.

"It's too dangerous. I can't see my hand in front of my face," Slocum said. "We might step into a deep hole. Caves near water like this sometimes have underground passages into the water. Step into a sinkhole like that, and you're a dead man.''

"It is dark," the professor conceded. "But the smell! Something lives in here."

Slocum backed away, wary of the intense darkness ahead. He joined the two researchers. His Colt Navy slid back into his holster.

"All manner of animals live along a lake," Slocum pointed out. "There's nothing to show it's your monster that lives here. Might be a badger or even something larger. A bear, maybe.''

"Dark Cloud said this was the place. He is certain the creature makes its lair here." The professor threw up his hands and turned in a circle as he studied the cave ceiling. "I *feel* it. This *is* the right place."

Slocum was edgy, but he had no sense they shared the cave with another living creature. He herded the professor and Polly back to the mouth and said, "If your monster's gone for the night, it won't be back until sunrise. There's no point in poking around.''

"We can find how it lives. There might be a nest," Polly said. "There might be eggs! Young ones!"

"We don't go back inside without a torch," Slocum said. He moved uneasily as he stepped on something that crunched under his feet. Eggs? He couldn't tell if Polly's suggestion made him consider that possibility or if the grating sound reminded him of sneaking through henhouses when he was a boy. "Prowling around without seeing where we're stepping is more than dangerous, it's downright foolish."

"Mr. Slocum is correct," the professor said with some reluctance. "That does not mean we don't have many other avenues of investigation to explore. We need to set up a camera nearby so we can photograph our quarry when it comes back at dawn."

"If it comes back," Slocum reminded the enthusiastic scholar. "I can see if there's evidence along the shoreline and up the slopes. Any creature that lives in a cave has to come and go, leaving spoor."

"A capital idea! You and Polly go in that direction," Malloy said, pointing out along the rocky outjut of land, "and I shall go the other way."

Slocum helped the blond across the rocky flats to the far side of the beach. He was aware of her nearness, but he also saw she barely noticed him. As excited as her mentor was, Polly Greene was even more delirious with the notion of tracking down a sea monster.

"What do we look for, John?" Polly asked. "I know nothing about tracking."

"An animal big enough to lair in the cave can't move without leaving tracks. If it slithers, it'll sink into the soft sand or mud. If it walks, footprints will give away its passage." Slocum went slowly, eyes studying the ground. The rocky area gave way to a sandy beach, washed smooth by the incessant wave motion. Near the end of the outjutting, he dropped to one knee and bent down.

"What is it?"

"Can't say I've ever seen anything like it," Slocum said. His fingers traced over a depression the size of a dinner plate. What might be claws dug down even deeper at one side, but the waves had erased much of the detail. It might have been nothing more than coincidence, some quirk formed on the beach and not left by a mammoth amphibian.

"If this is a footprint, your monster's the size of a house," Slocum said. "But there's no way of telling with only a single print." He cast about, going toward the water and then away as he sought more tracks. He found nothing but the solitary depression in the sand.

"This is important evidence," Polly said breathlessly. "It proves—"

"It proves nothing," Slocum cut in. "I couldn't swear that an animal made that mark. We've got to find more. Let's go back and see what the professor's unearthed."

They retraced their path to the cave mouth. Professor Malloy grunted and gasped as he dragged a large crate from the buckboard to the edge of the water.

"Professor, really!" exclaimed Polly. She stamped her foot and said, "You ought to have let Mr. Slocum and me help. It is too taxing to bring our equipment from camp."

"I had to set up right away. We dare not miss any sign of the creature," he said, ripping open the wooden crate and pulling out a tripod and camera. "I want to get a photograph."

"Doesn't that take a spell?" Slocum asked. He remembered seeing men sit for as long as ten minutes while their pictures were being taken. "If you open the lens, any animal would move right out of range before you caught its image."

"True, but I have an angle going from the rocky flats out into the lake. All I need are thirty seconds for the exposure. This is a special photographic plate developed by a scientist in New York City for such work." The professor hummed to himself as he set up the camera on its sturdy tripod.

Slocum sat down, aware of how tired he had become from struggling across the rocky beach. He stood and searched for Dark Cloud.

"Where's the Paiute?" Slocum asked, suddenly concerned. "I don't see him anywhere. Was he with you, professor?"

"What? Dark Cloud? No, he stayed here while I retrieved my camera equipment, or so I thought. He must be around. There's no reason for him to wander away."

"Do you see him anywhere, Polly?" Slocum asked in a low voice. He listened hard but heard nothing. If Dark Cloud was truly the scout who had ridden for Major Conroy, finding him would be harder than finding a ghost in the middle of a fog bank, if he wanted to hide. Somehow, Slocum didn't think that was what had happened. He had developed a sixth sense to warn of danger.

It was screaming at him now.

"I'm going to find him," he told Polly. "You help the professor."

"All right, John." He started from her, only to feel her fingers tighten on his arm. He turned back and gazed down into her gray eyes. She smiled, then rose up slightly and kissed him. "Thank you for all your help, John. I know you don't believe there's anything here. I appreciate what you're doing for us. *We* appreciate it."

"I'm getting paid well for it," Slocum said. He drew away and quickly melted into the darkness. The only way Dark Cloud could have left without him and Polly seeing him was back toward their camp or along the shoreline. Since the professor hadn't noticed the Paiute, Slocum felt sure Dark Cloud had walked along the water.

Less than fifty feet off, he found a moccasin print. The water worked to erase it, but Slocum saw he was heading in the right direction. Long legs devouring the distance, he hurried along the shore, occasionally noting a footprint in the sand. He reached a portion of the beach with few rocks—and no moccasin prints.

"Uphill?" Slocum turned and looked up the slope into the woods. What had drawn Dark Cloud there? Scouting back and forth over a long stretch of beach, Slocum finally found crushed grass showing where the Paiute had gone.

Before he could enter the dark, wooded area and track the Indian, a hideous scream cut through the still, night air. The animals moving about in the night froze, the chirping insects fell silent, and only the lap, lap, lap of the lake water vied with the blood-curdling cry. Slocum thought the cry came from ahead. But when the sound of a careless footstep behind reached him, he spun, drawing his six-gun as he went into a crouch.

Slocum relaxed when he saw Professor Malloy and Polly Greene. He eased down the hammer of the Colt and stood.

"You are very fast with your gun, Mr. Slocum," Malloy said in a tiny voice. "I had no idea you were so adept."

"Keeps me alive when people sneak up behind me," said Slocum. He shoved his six-shooter back into the cross-draw holster.

"We heard a scream," Polly said, her voice choked with fear. "What caused it? Some animal?"

"I don't think so. You folks might want to stay here and—"

"No!" Polly heaved a deep breath. "We might be in more danger alone than with you. We have no weapon."

Slocum saw how the professor clutched his walking stick and wondered if that were true. He suspected the scholar could use it as a club with deadly result.

"I don't know what's up there. It might not be pretty."

"We will be all right, sir," said Professor Malloy. He put his arm around Polly's waist and pulled her closer for comfort.

Slocum silently turned and started up the steep slope, stumbling now and again on the treacherous ground. Muddy stretches gave him some hint that Dark Cloud had preceded him, but the tracks were poor. All Slocum could really tell was that someone wearing moccasins had passed through recently.

At the top of the hill, Slocum got a good view of Bear Lake. With a rising crescent of moon, he caught sight of the waves moving slowly over the lake's surface. They were outlined in bright silver and showed fish jumping out to catch low-flying insects. Everything was as it ought to be on the lake.

Slocum quickly found evidence that things were not as

they should be along the ridge. Something huge had been dragged along the top, disturbing weeds and snapping off flowers. He dropped down and decided that whatever had passed through had gone toward the copse ahead. Lodgepole pines and junipers grew close together to make an impenetrably dark forest.

With Professor Malloy and Polly struggling up the slope, Slocum hurried off. Polly called for him to stop. He didn't want her to see what he feared he would find. The closer he got to the woods, the more he suspected foul play. Even as alert as he was, Slocum almost stumbled over Dark Cloud's body.

Slocum recoiled and stepped away. His gorge rose. He fought it down. During the war he had seen men blown apart by cannon fire, pieces blasted off by minié balls, death and maiming of all description. Seldom had he seen a man mauled as badly as Dark Cloud.

"John, what—oh, dear God!"

Polly buried her face in Slocum's shoulder. Hot tears burned into his shirt. He spun her around to keep her from getting any better view of the corpse. Professor Malloy stepped around, then dropped down to examine Dark Cloud.

"Ripped apart," the professor said in a level voice. He might have been delivering a lecture to his class at Harvard. "Huge claws, from the way the wounds start on the chest and rake downward. Gutted. Dark Cloud was gutted and—"

"Professor," cautioned Slocum. He moved Polly away and said softly to her, "Just stay back and let us see what happened."

"It's the monster," she sobbed out. "The monster killed him!"

Slocum stood over the professor as the academic worked on Dark Cloud's body, rolling it from side to side. Whatever had mauled the Paiute had struck quickly.

"He didn't have a chance," Slocum said. "I heard only the one cry, then nothing. He died quick."

"It would seem so," Professor Malloy said. "I can come to no conclusion about the agent causing such wounds. Are there bears large enough to do such injury?"

"Reckon so. A bear wouldn't leave so quick, though. Grizzlies don't usually eat people. We're too tough and maybe taste bad, but a bear wouldn't just wander off." Slocum began working around in a broad circle. He saw no spoor from a bear or anything else large enough to kill Dark Cloud so quickly. Even debilitated as he was by consumption, Dark Cloud could have put up a fight, given the chance. He wore a knife at his belt and no man who had saved Major Conroy's troop, taking four arrows doing it and still fighting on, would succumb so easily.

"Find anything?" called Polly. She stood where Slocum had left her, arms wrapped around her quaking body.

"Nothing," he admitted. "There's only one rocky patch leading that way where a bear—or any other animal—might have run without leaving tracks." The direction he indicated led over the ridge and down the far side, away from the lake. If the professor was right about a creature living in Bear Lake, it ought to return to its habitat after a kill. Slocum would swear on a stack of Bibles nothing big had sneaked past him going back to the shore.

"It's the monster," Polly said, her teeth chattering now. "It *must* be!"

"If you follow the top of the ridge around and not go down to the lake, you'll reach where we set up camp and left the buckboard," Slocum said. "And it's also in the opposite direction taken by whatever did that to Dark Cloud."

"We ought to take him back to Corinne for the authorities," Malloy said. "An investigation is required."

"Do you think anyone in Corinne is going to give a bucket of warm spit about a Paiute being killed?" Slocum shook his head. "He might have saved the hides of an entire company of cavalry, but nobody cares."

"We can contact the cavalry. Perhaps they will desire a military funeral."

"They might," Slocum said, anxious to hunt down whatever had done the killing. "You get Polly away from here and wait for me to return."

"We can load the body into the buckboard. It won't take long to get the team and return here. There might be a road along the top of the ridge."

"I doubt it. Not too many come this way," Slocum said. His fingers tapped on the butt of his six-shooter. "You head on back. I want to find what went on here."

"Be careful, Mr. Slocum."

Slocum stepped to one side of the rocky area where he suspected the killer had fled. He walked to the other side and decided the area wasn't wide enough for a big monster, not like the one described by the townsfolk. Crisscrossing to find any trace of the assailant, Slocum saw occasional black droplets. In the moonlight, blood always showed dark as pitch. He walked faster, the woods surrounding him with fragrance and utter quiet.

Slocum almost turned and went back to join the professor and Polly Greene. He wasn't the kind to spook easily, but something silenced the usual night sounds in the woods. Waiting almost two minutes didn't bring back the sounds he expected. Something other than his own passage caused the caution among the woods dwellers.

He went deeper into the woods, keen eyes looking for any signs of a large animal. He saw nothing to indicate that a beast large enough to gut Dark Cloud had come this way.

He pushed on, moving faster when he discovered a few broken twigs along a game path. The incline under him showed he was heading down the far side of the hill protecting Bear Lake. The path began twisting and turning, splitting into several routes taken by the animals. At every fork, Slocum tried to decide which way Dark Cloud's killer might have gone.

He worked more by instinct than visual clues. And when he heard a sound of something heavy crunching down on dried pine needles, he jerked around. The movement caused Slocum to stumble on a large rock, and he fell heavily.

Slocum scrambled to get back to his feet—then he froze.

A telltale noise sounded as loud as a trumpet of doom. Slocum stared down the bore of a cocked, double-barreled shotgun.

6

Slocum's mind raced. He had his six-shooter in his hand, but he could not swing it about to get the gunman in his sights. Not in time. Not with a shotgun already cocked and stuck smack-dab in his face.

"Hold on!" Slocum called, hoping he wouldn't be killed outright. "Don't go doing anything you'll regret."

A cold chuckle sounded like a peal of doom to Slocum. "Ain't nothin' *I'll* regret. You're gonna be the dead one, not me."

Slocum scooted back and sat up, considering his chances of firing and hitting anything. He couldn't.

"Put that hogleg of yours down and move away from it." The barrels of the shotgun jerked to one side, showing where Slocum was supposed to go.

He obeyed. He had no other choice. Only when the man moved from deep shadows did Slocum see him.

"You bought me a drink back in Corinne," Slocum said, trying to find common ground. "You're the miner who struck it rich. Tork Beckwourth!"

"That's the name, mister," Beckwourth said, stooping to scoop up Slocum's Colt. He tucked it into his belt. "I remember you. You was outside the assay office when me and

61

Gold Tooth came out. What are you doin' out here? You ain't thinkin' to jump our claim, are you?''

"No," Slocum said earnestly. He cautiously got to his feet. The double-barreled shotgun never left him. A light pull would send one barrel of buckshot ripping through him. If Beckwourth tensed enough, both barrels would be fired point-blank into his body. Slocum had thought Dark Cloud was mauled. The shotgun would turn him into ground meat.

"Get movin'. That way, down the path. Don't try anything funny or I'll plug you."

"I'm no claim jumper. I don't even know where your claim is."

"You coulda found out. The yahoo in the land office knows. Most everybody in Corinne knows where we work. What else would you be doin' out here in the middle of the night?"

Slocum knew better than to mention the professor or Polly. Tork Beckwourth had an itchy finger and a suspicious mind. He might take it into his head to go take them prisoners. A woman as pretty as Polly Greene would inspire a ruthless miner to acts Slocum didn't care to think on much. If he could help her escape such a fate, he would.

"The monster. I'm trying to find the monster everybody in town's talking about."

"What are they sayin'? Who's spreadin' them lies? There's no such thing as a monster. Not in Bear Lake, at any rate."

Slocum kept walking, not answering directly. "You know how rumors build up and boil over. A fellow named Wallings was—"

"Wallings!" roared Beckwourth. "I ought to cut you down where you stand. That lyin', self-servin' son of a bitch. I ain't got any more use for him than I do for a four-card flush. You and him ain't thrown in together, have you?"

"No, I just got into town. Haven't made any friends, especially not Wallings.'' Slocum felt like his mouth was running away with his mind. He had to convince the miner he wasn't a threat to the claim. ''What were you doing out in the forest, waiting by a game trail?''

''Hunting,'' came the laconic answer. That Beckwourth didn't add any more made Slocum even more suspicious. He wasn't certain whatever had killed Dark Cloud had come down the trail where Beckwourth waited in hiding, but it might have. The miner might have been responsible for the hideous death visited upon the Paiute scout. That didn't make Slocum any more comfortable being the hard rock miner's prisoner.

''Don't go that way. Over to the cabin.'' Beckwourth poked Slocum in the middle of the back with the hard barrel. Slocum veered away from the side of the hill, past a long line of mine tailings, to a small line shack. A lantern burned dimly inside, but it gave more light than Slocum's eyes could handle at first.

Beckwourth shoved him to one side. Slocum sat down heavily on the dirt floor. The miner settled onto one of two beds at the far end of the cabin. The burly man obviously turned over and over some weighty thought. Slocum hoped he wouldn't hurt himself by thinking too hard.

''Don't rightly know what to do with you. I don't think Wallings sent you to spy on us. You weren't good enough.''

''I didn't even know you were here. As I said, I was out hunting for the creature that lives in the lake.''

Beckwourth snorted, then stood and went to the door. He held the shotgun on Slocum. Getting to his feet and knocking the weapon aside was impossible. Slocum would be cut in half before he got anywhere near the miner. Tork Beckwourth thrust his head outside and talked to somebody. Slocum caught only a part of the query.

''. . . what we gonna do with him? Can't up and kill him

without causin' somebody to come askin' after his worthless carcass.''

The whispered answer eluded Slocum.

"How much longer?" Beckwourth asked. "That long? Hell, what are we gonna do with him?"

Slocum edged around to sneak a look through the opening between hinges and door. The dilapidated shack provided more cracks and spy holes than Slocum could use. He saw a dark form outside but couldn't make out the identity of whom Beckwourth argued with.

"Don't get any funny ideas," Beckwourth said, lifting the barrel of the shotgun and training it squarely on Slocum. The shotgun had drifted a tad off target. Beckwourth turned back to his conversation. All Slocum heard was, "Well, get them out here. We can't take all day!"

Beckwourth slammed the door and dropped to the bunk, glowering at Slocum. Conversation was out of the question. Slocum heard Beckwourth's partner moving around outside, then stalking off.

He didn't know how long they sat, but the first light of dawn finally shed more illumination than the dirty kerosene lamp sputtering on the table.

"You need to trim your wick," Slocum finally said. Beckwourth snapped around. Slocum hadn't realized the man was more asleep than awake. If he had known, he might have tried jumping Beckwourth.

"Getting near dawn," Beckwourth said, rubbing his nose across his sleeve. He stood, the shotgun never straying far from Slocum. The miner kicked open the cabin door and looked out. "Jehosophat!" Beckwourth jumped as if a fire had been lit under his butt. He swung around and motioned for Slocum to stand.

"I don't know what they got in mind for you, but it won't be purty. We don't cotton to no claim jumpers."

Slocum moved in response to Beckwourth's shotgun

movement. "Who are you including in that? Wasn't that Gold Tooth you talked to earlier?"

"No questions." Beckwourth seemed edgier than before. Slocum took his time walking in the direction Beckwourth prodded him. He got a better view of the mine. The tailings stretched out a hundred yards down the hill, but they didn't strike Slocum as being heavy enough for a mine drilled halfway through the hill.

"The powder shed. Get into it."

The blasting powder storage shed had a sturdier door on it than the cabin. The heavy hasp and lock showed Beckwourth and his partner kept their valuables here. As Slocum turned, Beckwourth shoved him hard. For a brief instant, Slocum caught sight of a carriage rattling up the slope toward the mine opening. A ray of pure gold shone from a man riding a horse next to the wagon.

"Gold Tooth's bringing visitors," Slocum said to himself.

"What's that?" Tork Beckwourth shoved Slocum down and rolled him onto his belly. Seizing a length of rope, the big miner quickly bound Slocum's wrists. Finished, he dropped a couple loops around Slocum's ankles and cinched it up tight. "That'll hold you. Don't go gettin' any ideas about escapin'. We'll shoot you where you stand."

"Who's 'we'?" Slocum asked. "You and Lawton and who else?"

He shut up when he saw the expression on the miner's face. It wasn't fear; it wasn't anger. It combined both mixed in with a dollop of slyness, as if Slocum had asked the question Tork Beckwourth was most likely to lie about when answering.

"We won't leave you alone too long. We'll be back." Beckwourth slammed the door, plunging Slocum into darkness. The miner fumbled with the lock, taking several seconds to get it snapped shut.

Slocum kicked, rolled onto his back, then wiggled until he

could sit upright. The rough-planked wall behind him, he shifted back and forth until he was more comfortable. He hadn't liked the way the miner promised to return. When he did, it was likely to be with a couple loads of buckshot. Why Beckwourth hadn't killed him outright, Slocum wasn't sure, but he thought it might have something to do with the men who had ridden up with Gold Tooth Lawton.

Pressing his face against the wall, he found a crack large enough to peer out. He didn't see anyone moving around at the end of the tailings. Slocum twisted and found a knothole. This gave a better view. Two men talked with Tork Beckwourth and Gold Tooth Lawton—and someone else hid nearby. Slocum caught sight of the man crouched behind an overturned ore cart, spying on the miners and the two well-dressed men with them.

"Haskell," hissed Slocum, recognizing the man snooping on the foursome. "I might have known you were mixed up in this. You have your thumb stuck into damned near everything."

Slocum's cheek began itching from the rough wood. He tried to scratch it and couldn't. He sagged to one side, hitting a large box. Squirming around, Slocum pressed the ropes lashed around his wrists into the crate. Rubbing briskly, he felt the strands parting slowly. He had not been too worried about escaping. Beckwourth hadn't done a good job hogtying him. Sweat running down his face and making it itch even worse, Slocum kept at the sawing until the last strand parted.

He heaved a sigh of relief, rubbed his wrists, then scratched vigorously. Another minute saw him free of the ropes around his ankles. Then Slocum pressed hard against the shed wall again to watch what transpired.

The well-dressed men continued to talk, pointing this way and that, mostly into the mine shaft. Tork Beckwourth and Gold Tooth Lawton tried to get a word wedged in but the others wouldn't listen. Finally, the two miners fell silent. Slocum saw how they fumed—and he also saw how antsy Joe Haskell became.

"Hardy!" shouted one of the businessmen. "Get on out here."

From the mouth of the mine came a grizzled old-timer. Slocum recognized a hard rock miner when he saw one. Hardy had been working the stopes for a long time. He carried two large rocks from the mine. He tossed one to each of the businessmen.

"Can't rightly see what the fuss is about," Hardy said, his gravelly voice catching on a morning breeze and coming Slocum's way. "No blue dirt in this mine."

"What?" raged Beckwourth. "You son of a bitch. You lyin'—" He started for Hardy, who stepped back and reached for a rock hammer stuck into his belt.

The businessmen spoke in tones too low for Slocum to hear, but they separated the men. Then they left, Hardy trailing along, grumbling and waving his rock hammer in Beckwourth's direction. The miner started after Hardy, but Gold Tooth Lawton held his partner back.

Slocum moved to another crack and saw the businessmen climb into the wagon, Hardy jumping into the bed behind them. They wasted no time in turning around and snapping the reins on their horses' rumps, getting the team moving downhill and away from the mine.

Slocum heard a hubbub from the mine shaft and returned to the crack giving him the best view. Beckwourth and Lawton had lit into each other, fists swinging in powerful haymakers that would have felled an elephant had any landed. The two miners fought clumsily, then grappled, crashing to the ground and rolling over and over.

"You son of a bitch. You done ruined everything!" shouted one.

"Me? Me? You lop-eared galoot. I didn't run them fellas

off. You did. You're the one what ruined everything.''

Beckwourth and Lawton rolled over and over, kicking up a cloud of dust. One—Slocum couldn't get a clear view—picked up a rock and tried to crush his partner's skull. All that stopped him was Haskell's quick intervention. He had raced from behind the rusty ore cart and grabbed the upraised rock, wresting it from angry hands.

''Stop it, you two. We don't get anywhere arguin' among ourselves. Stop it!'' Haskell whipped out his six-shooter and fired a round into the air. When the two miners didn't stop their fight, Haskell fired again. This got their attention because he had triggered the round into the ground next to them.

''You ain't got no call doin' that, Haskell,'' grumbled Beckwourth. The giant miner growled and started to swing at Lawton again, but the smaller miner scrambled away out of range. He got to his feet, stance wide and ready for more fisticuffs.

Haskell stepped between them and spoke in a calming voice. His words vanished as Slocum tried to make them out. He wondered what was happening, but whatever it was, nobody outside was happy. The two well-dressed men had brought an expert miner with them and Hardy's decision hadn't set well.

Slocum pushed back from the wall, realizing it wouldn't be long before they remembered their prisoner and came for him. The long shotgun Beckwourth carried would put too many holes in Slocum's hide ever to be patched. He pushed hard against the shed door, but the lock and hinges held securely.

Working around, Slocum finally found a loose plank in the wall. He kicked at it, trying not to make too much noise, which would bring the trio down on him like flies to shit. Nails screeched as he tore the wood away. A second plank pulled free and then part of a third. Slocum broke off the remainder as he wiggled through the wall, falling into the dust outside the shed.

He smiled wryly. If he hadn't been able to get free, a single lucifer tossed into the kegs of blasting powder would have taken care of anybody coming to kill him. He would have been blown to kingdom come, too, but taking at least one of those owlhoots with him would have been satisfying.

Now he had the chance to wring all three of their necks. Slocum peered around the shed, wondering if the noise he'd made had drawn their attention. He didn't see them. Keeping low, he dashed across an open area and dived belly down behind timbers cut to support the roof of the mine. He crawled forward and got a look at the overturned ore cart.

Haskell was nowhere to be seen. Neither of the mine owners showed their faces, either. Slocum got up and tried to locate them. He heard nothing and he saw nothing. Curious, he made his way back down the slope and cautiously looked into the cabin. Empty.

A slow smile crossed his lips. Beckwourth had left Slocum's Colt Navy on the table. Slocum ducked inside, grabbed his six-gun, and immediately checked the cylinder. Fully loaded. He could take the three of them with no trouble. Haskell was a bad shot, Gold Tooth Lawton didn't carry a hogleg, and Tork Beckwourth's shotgun didn't amount to a hill of beans if Slocum got the miner in his sights first.

"Where the hell did you all go?" Slocum wondered aloud as he scouted the area. It was as if the earth had opened up and swallowed the three men. He scratched his cheek again, then turned toward the gaping mouth of the mine.

"Hell, Hardy found something in there. No reason I can't, also." Slocum kept to cover as he made his way up the steep slope to the mine shaft. He paused for a moment, scanning the terrain below the opening. Still no sign of the two miners and Joe Haskell. Slocum tucked his pistol back into his holster, ducked, and entered the mine.

A carbide lamp rested on the shelf to his right. Slocum sloshed the water around a mite, then ignited the brilliant lamp, casting a purple white beam of light deep into the mine. The ore cart tracks were rusted and crooked.

"Can't move too much ore on those rails," he decided. He hunched over and moved farther into the mine. There were several places where fresh nicks showed samples being picked out of the walls. The rock around the samples didn't appear too promising for gold or silver.

The musty odor of a closed mine grew stronger. Slocum worried about running into mine gas but decided Beckwourth and Lawton hadn't died, so he wouldn't, either. Here and there he found evidence of new digging done by a rock hammer.

"Hardy was busy here," he decided. But the rock wasn't ore bearing. A few more steps into the mine caused Slocum to let out a low whistle. Everywhere he looked sparkled gold. He held up the lamp and studied one nugget, then reached out to touch it.

He froze when he heard timbers creaking ominously. Then an explosion lifted him off his feet and threw him deeper into the mine. Dust choked him and the only light reaching his eyes came from the carbide lamp.

Trapped!

7

Slocum coughed until he thought his lungs would come out and then wiped grit from his eyes. For a terrifying instant, he thought he had gone blind. Finally his eyes watered enough for him to get the last of the dirt out. The carbide lamp still glowed as brightly as ever. The pall of powdered earth hanging suspended in the mine shaft turned everything a uniform shade of gray in the light—and beyond loomed only Stygian darkness.

Slocum coughed again and used his bandanna to wipe away the grime. Then he fastened the cloth around his nose and mouth to help him breathe. He knew there was no chance of finding water in the mine to soak the bandanna, but even dry, the filtering helped.

Swinging the carbide light around, Slocum went cold inside. He was trapped in a tiny chamber, hardly long enough for him to take three strides before bumping into a wall. From his earliest childhood he had been leery of caves. He and his brother Robert had once been trapped in a cave-in as they played back in Calhoun, Georgia. They had managed to dig their way out through soft dirt at the top of the fall and neither had told their father. The elder Slocum would have whipped them good for even daring to enter such an unsafe place.

Right about now, Slocum wished he could hear his father's voice telling him not to do anything as damnfool stupid as going into a mine without knowing who was left outside. Haskell might have set off the blast to kill him, but Slocum knew Gold Tooth Lawton and Tork Beckwourth were equally capable.

"Maybe they didn't realize anybody was even in here," he muttered to himself. Already the air turned a bit stuffy. Or was it only his imagination working on him? Slocum forced down fear and tried not to panic. Doing so would only bring about his death that much faster.

Stumbling across the debris from the cave-in, he got to the rock plugging the mouth. He made a few attempts to move stones, but most of the fall was big, heavy rock requiring a pick and shovel and more time than he likely had. He wiped away the sweat running into his eyes and knew the wavering of his vision would only get worse.

"No food or water," he said to himself. "No air. If I can't get out of here, I'll suffocate." Again, a heavy weight crushed down on his chest, but Slocum knew it was only fear. His active imagination made the situation worse than it was—for the moment.

He kept trying to pull loose enough stone to break free a tunnel to the outside. Any air entering would help, even if he had to push his nose against the opening and suck it in that way.

Ten minutes of futile digging convinced him the explosion had brought down close to ten feet of roof. There was no way in hell he was going to move that much rock with his bare hands.

Disgusted but not daunted, Slocum slid down the slope of the rock barring his exit. He turned his attention back into the mine, where he hadn't had time to explore before the cave-in. Going to the back of the chamber, he pushed against the obstruction caused by the blast. To his surprise, it yielded easily, falling out to the other side. He scooted through the hole and tumbled into the shaft beyond.

Holding the carbide light aloft, he saw the tunnel stretching far back into the hillside. A considerable amount of the tunnel seemed to be natural fissure, accounting for the lack of tailings he had noticed outside. Slocum was no mining engineer, but he knew it was odd for a crack to form along a vein of gold. The precious mineral always drove right through the hardest rock, making recovery a backbreaking chore. It was as if Mother Nature insisted on killing labor to steal her most precious substance.

Slocum worked his way along the natural rift, noting how the vein of gold dipped into the wall and returned. He frowned when he saw how often this happened. Again, he wasn't an expert, but he had heard enough real miners cussing over how gold always took off in a vein straight away opposite from the direction of their digging. Seldom did it wander back and forth, unless there were two distinct veins.

"The whole damned mine's not valuable enough for there to be two veins running through it." He continued along the rift, wondering where Tork Beckwourth had found the big nugget he had flashed around Corinne the night before. The width of the vein of blue dirt—if it was even high assay ore—was hardly thicker than a knife blade. Slocum dug his thumbnail into it and came away with only a faint silvery smear.

Shaking his head, he knew anyone working this mine would be in for hard work and little return. But where had Beckwourth's nugget come from, if not this hole?

Slocum held up the carbide lamp when he felt a faint puff of wind across his face.

"Air! Fresh air! A vent!" He looked around but didn't find the opening he so eagerly sought. Calming, he hunkered down and thought for a moment. He reached over and turned down the intensely white light of the lamp until it was little more than a dull glow. Closing his eyes, Slocum waited for almost a minute.

He thought it must have stretched to eternity. But when he opened his dark-adapted eyes, the faint glimmering of daylight came to him immediately. A tiny chimney, hardly wider than his forearm, opened off the natural rift. More than thirty feet separated him from the surface, but Slocum never hesitated. He forced his way into the chimney and began slithering toward the distant opening. He hadn't gone more than a few feet when a sickening realization hit him.

The vent might provide air, but it could never give him freedom. The heavy rock around him was too solid to dig. Not a single loose stone gave him even an extra inch to slide forward. With his shoulders firmly wedged into the vent, he had no chance of going farther.

Disheartened, he forced his way back down into the mine, landing on the floor amid a cloud of dust. Slocum panted heavily from the exertion of his climb. He hadn't gotten even halfway. Barely six feet, he reckoned, his boots hardly leaving the mine shaft.

"Dammit," he swore. He leaned back against the wall and stared straight up at the tormenting light dancing along the mouth of the vent. So near and yet it might as well have been on the other side of the Mississippi River for all the good it did him.

"Got air." He sighed. Then he fell silent. Something nagged at him. It took several seconds for him to realize that the vibrations he felt in the rock weren't naturally occurring.

"Beckwourth and Lawton. They're trying to open the mine!" Slocum shot to his feet and stumbled along the littered mine floor back to the plug in the mouth of the shaft. He shouted for them to continue. No answer. He pressed his hand against the rock, thinking to feel heavier vibration from their digging.

"What?" Slocum backed off and stared. He detected no

sign of digging. This close to the mouth, he should have felt every impact of pick and every scrape of shovel. But there was nothing. Nothing at all.

Puzzled, Slocum pressed his ear against a large rock. Again he heard distant vibration, but it wasn't coming from this direction. He pushed back and stared into the depths of the mine. The answer lay at the back of the shaft, not the mouth. Carefully picking his way past the vent he had thought promised him escape, he kept going deeper into the mine. Here and there large chunks of rock had been blown out and mucked away, but the rift proved more natural than dug by Beckwourth or Lawton.

And the vibration increased.

Slocum stopped to turn up the carbide lamp, but it sizzled and hissed and died. He turned up the light even more. When it began sputtering, the cold truth hit him. The water in the lamp was about gone. All too soon he would be in the dark, left to die of thirst and starvation.

"Help me!" he shouted. For a moment, the echoes came back, mingled with the dull droning of vibration through the rock. Then all Slocum heard was his own breathing. Silence like that of the grave met him. He pressed his ear against the stony wall.

Silence. No vibration. No hint that anyone dug to get him out. And the carbide lamp finally gasped and sizzled to a black death.

John Slocum wasn't a quitter, but his hand drifted toward the Colt Navy in its holster. Better a bullet than to die like a dog in the mine. But as his eyes adapted once more to the utter darkness, he noted a shaft of light ahead. Thinking he had gotten turned around in the mine, Slocum spun around. The faint ray from the vent where he had tried to climb out dropped to the floor in a dusty column.

Slocum swung back and walked slowly in the dark toward the brighter, thicker ray of light coming from above. He stopped under a second vent. This one was wider, almost too wide for him. Slocum jumped up, grabbed hold of a rocky outjut, then forced his way into the chimney. He had to shove his feet against the far side of the chimney, his back getting scraped as he inched upward. But as slow as the ascent was, hope grew with every passing minute.

Fingers bleeding, he reached up and caught the jagged edge of the rock barring him from getting free. The chimney had closed up so much, Slocum was bent almost double, but he hardly noticed as he scrabbled to pull away rock. The hillside resisted his efforts, but he remembered how he had feared he would be trapped forever in the plugged-up mine.

Slocum was never sure what he did, but he succeeded in prying loose a rock that tumbled down and hit him in the face. Then he saw freedom staring at him. Forcing through the opening, he fell heavily on the rock and lay in the sunlight, soaking up the rays like a lizard on a warm spring day.

He rolled over and stared at the clear sky, only a few white puffy clouds moving slowly toward the south. The trees gave him the first decent breath of air he'd had since being caught in the mine shaft, and the feel of dirt under his boots made him want to cry for joy.

Then he rubbed his bleeding hands on his jeans and began to feel the ache in his back. The ache turned to a dull, throbbing pain where he had abraded his skin climbing the chimney. Even his strong legs hurt from the cramped position in the ascent. With the growing awareness of his injuries, Slocum also felt a mounting need to plug the son of a bitch who had trapped him.

"An explosion. Somebody tossed a stick of dynamite into the tunnel to kill me," he said, turning around to get his bearings. He had come over the crest of the hill. He hiked up and started down the other side, heading for Beckwourth's and Lawton's camp. He thought Joe Haskell might have had a hand in it. The murderous drifter had thrown in with the two miners in some deal that probably spelled fraud. Slocum hadn't overheard enough of the discussion between the two well-dressed men and their mining expert, but it sounded as if Beckwourth and Lawton had tried to sell a salted mine.

"That's Haskell's style," Slocum decided as he slipped and slid down the increasingly steep face of the hill. He came to a halt just above the miners' camp. Drawing his Colt, he scanned the terrain for a good target. He wasn't above putting a couple of slugs in each of the men for trying to kill him. It was their due.

Slocum shielded his eyes against the lowering sun. For a moment, Slocum wondered if something had gone wrong. Then he pulled out his brother Robert's watch and popped open the cover. It was almost five o'clock. He had spent most of the day trapped in the mine. The lack of light and the long climb had made time move in fitful spurts and starts.

Settling down, Slocum waited another ten minutes, but no one showed in the camp. He found a way down to the gunpowder shed where they had kept him prisoner. Empty. And their run-down cabin was similarly unoccupied. It was as if the men had decided to take the day off and had simply left for town. Slocum checked the mouth of the mine.

From the tons of rock that had crashed down, he wondered how he could have ever thought they were digging him out. It would take days of expert blasting to move most of that rock. New timbers would be needed for the roof and more rock had to be excavated before the main shaft could be reopened. That would take more effort than Slocum thought either Beckwourth or his partner wanted to expend.

Making his way back up the hill, he reached the crest and tried to figure out where he had left the professor and Polly Greene so many hours ago. They must think he had abandoned them. Trudging through the forest, he found the game trail where Beckwourth had snared him so easily. Occasional heel prints from his own boots told Slocum he was moving in the right direction. An hour later, as dusk was falling, he reached the place where Dark Cloud had died.

The smell warned him of the dead Paiute before he actually saw the blanket-covered body. Dark Cloud had been left exposed all day in the hot sun and had turned gamy. Slocum wondered why Professor Malloy hadn't fetched the buckboard and taken the Indian back to Corinne as he had intended.

Coldness formed in the pit of Slocum's belly. The only reason the scholar wouldn't keep his word on something that serious had to mean bigger trouble had blown in.

He started in the direction of the buckboard, only to slow and finally come to a complete halt. Professor Malloy and Polly were tenderfeet. They couldn't hide their trail if they tried. And Slocum had not seen any trace they had come this way. Returning to Dark Cloud's body, Slocum worked his way out in an ever-enlarging spiral. When he came across the petite footprint left by Polly's shoe, he knew they had not gone to the buckboard.

"Downhill, back to the lake," Slocum said, kneeling as he studied the print. It had been clearly imprinted in mud and slowly baked during the day. Not far off, Slocum found two more, belonging to Polly and her professor. Making his way slowly to the lake, he scouted the trail on either side to be sure no one herded them as captives or followed them. He found no sign of another human other than Polly and Malloy.

This thought made Slocum stop and consider something else. If the monster from Bear Lake had climbed up to maul Dark Cloud, it ought to have left a path big enough for a blind man to follow. Slocum saw no sign of a huge, lumbering beast—or even a smaller, two-legged one, other than the pair he tracked.

Slocum reached the shoreline and took a few minutes to determine the direction the professor and Polly Greene had taken. He hiked for only a few minutes before he saw two silhouettes moving along the water ahead of him.

"Professor!" he called, recognizing the small man's outline. "Polly! Are you all right?"

"Mr. Slocum!" Professor Malloy turned and waved his walking stick in way of greeting. "We thought you had left us."

"Got into a spot of trouble," Slocum said.

"A spot? My goodness, you're a fright!" exclaimed Polly. She ran her fingers over his tattered shirt, jerking away when he winced. She had pressed into his shredded skin and it hurt like hellfire. "You need patching up right away."

"Why didn't you take Dark Cloud's body back to Corinne? You should have been in town by now."

"We started back for the buckboard," the professor said, "but we got only a short distance before we . . . heard it."

"The creature in the lake! We heard it!" Polly bubbled over with enthusiasm. "We know how important it is to get Dark Cloud back to town, but the creature!"

"It was more important," Slocum said.

"Exactly," said Professor Malloy. "We had to come to the lake to catch sight of it. And we did."

"What? You *saw* it?"

"We did, John," Polly said, unable to restrain herself. "Rather, we think we might have. Out in the lake. Something rose up and curled down, two lumps following that might have been part of its body."

"It swam slowly and we only caught a glimpse of it. We've been sitting on the shore all day waiting for it to return."

Slocum scratched his head. Maybe the two had been in the sun too long. Sunstroke made people see things that weren't there, and both the professor and his student wanted to see the monster more than anything in the world. One might have witnessed ripples and convinced the other it was the monster.

"We set up our camera and waited for it to return to its lair—the nest we explored with you," Malloy said. "So far, the creature has not put in another appearance."

"Don't reckon it will, either," Slocum said, sure that he was right about heat exhaustion burning both their brains.

"Why do you say that, John?" Polly sounded aggrieved, as if she thought he accused her of outright lying.

"Didn't mean much by it. Strange things are going on around the lake," Slocum said, remembering Beckwourth, Lawton, and Haskell's dealings. "I just don't cotton much to the notion that there really is any monster in the lake."

A mournful bellow drifted across the lake. Slocum jerked around. In the distance he saw a dark shape rise from the water. For the world it appeared to be the head of a giant reptile. Another baleful lament sounded and the dark shape slipped back under the water of Bear Lake.

"Now, John, now do you believe us? That was the creature!" Polly had seen it, and Professor Malloy rushed to his fancy camera equipment to get its picture.

Slocum had seen it, but he still couldn't believe it.

8

Slocum's hand went for his six-shooter. He drew and cocked as he aimed. A hand hit his, knocking the gun up and away. The shot rang through the stillness of the twilight and the foot-long tongue of flame leaping from the six-gun's muzzle momentarily dazzled Slocum.

"Why'd you do that?" he demanded, swinging on Polly Greene. She stood beside him, pale and shaking.

"You can't hurt it, John. We must study the creature. It's the only way."

Slocum jerked around, hunting for the ripples in the water. He saw nothing, not the dark lumpy outline or any trace it had ever existed. Just when he thought it had all been a figment of his imagination, of wanting to see what Professor Malloy and Polly already had, he heard the melancholy song once more. It rose, quavered, then died until only silence reigned.

For several seconds Slocum heard nothing but the pounding of his own heart in his ears. Then, slowly, timidly, the usual sounds of night along the lakeshore returned. Fish jumped from the water in search of low-flying insects. Animals moved timorously at the waterside to drink and prowl, hunting for dinner and being hunted. And the fluttering of bats showed those nocturnal residents had no fear of whatever lived in Bear Lake.

"Where did it go?" Slocum demanded, still angry that Polly had stopped him from firing accurately. The distance was extreme for a handgun, but Slocum felt the need to try. He wanted to get a response from the poorly seen hulk, a cry of anger or even an attack. He shuddered. What if it were a monster and took it into its head to choose its dinner among the humans tormenting it?

"You ruined the picture, Mr. Slocum," Professor Malloy said, returning from his camera tripod. "I attempted to photograph it but was too late. Then you fired. I fear only a smear of flame will cut across the picture, totally obliterating the creature."

"What is it?" Slocum refused to give up. He had been through too much to take any guff from the scholar or his student. "How far away was it?"

"You think to bag it for dinner, Mr. Slocum?" Professor Malloy laughed as he tapped his walking stick against a rock on the ground. "It was across the lake. Your weapon could never reach that distance, and if it did, I believe the shot would have been, at best, annoying. That creature is a remnant of a former age, an epoch when tremendously huge beasts roamed."

"We have to trap it," Polly said eagerly. "We can do it. We know where its lair is. A net, a few stakes driven into the ground, we—"

"If it is as large as the professor claims," cut in Slocum, "it will take more than a net to capture it." His thoughts turned more to a buffalo rifle. A tripod-mounted Sharps .50 carried enough stopping power to bring down any creature, even if it was the size of an elephant.

"A net woven from steel wire," Polly rattled on. "We can dangle it down across the mouth of the lair, trapping it inside. We don't need to find a cage for it that way."

"No, my dear," said Professor Malloy, "that will not do. We need to study it as it goes about its natural daily rituals. Only in this way can we learn the most about it. Simply putting it in a cage, on display, might give us some notoriety, but our knowledge will be abridged. We must think of obtaining complete information concerning it. Yes, yes." The professor rubbed his chin as he turned back to his camera equipment. He muttered to himself as he changed plates, putting the one from the camera into a special container and then reloading the camera with a new photographic plate.

"I want to see it closer," Slocum said. He returned his six-shooter to his holster. Wishing he still had the carbide lamp from the mine or a similar lantern to cast some light on the treacherously rocky stretch ahead of him, Slocum started. He took only two steps before Polly grabbed his arm.

"Wait, John, let me go with you. I know more about the creature and its habits than you."

"How's that?"

"Well, I have studied similar ancient creatures. That matters more than anything else." He knew telling her to remain would have no effect. She was like a hound scenting its quarry. She would rush out without him if he denied her now. Slocum decided it was better to have her in sight rather than having to track her down in the dark if she got lost— or worse. She might actually find the monster and discover she had provided it with an early dinner.

"Come along, but you have to keep up," Slocum said. He cast a quick glance in Malloy's direction. The professor contented himself with scanning the lake, waiting for any ripple betraying the creature's presence. He had no time for his assistant.

"Where were you, John? We were so worried, and you look awful." Again she tried to brush off some of the dust he had accumulated. He pulled away when she touched the scrapes he had garnered getting free of the mine.

As they walked, Slocum told her what he could about his kidnapping and the attempted murder.

"Did they know you were inside the mine? How terrible!"

"I don't know if they knew. They had to know I had escaped from the powder shed." As they picked their way along the edge of Bear Lake, Slocum's thoughts went back to Beckwourth and Lawton's mine and the explosion. He wasn't sure who had tossed the dynamite into the mine mouth. It might have been the miners, or it could have been Haskell. Joe Haskell owed him nothing but sorrow. Slocum decided he should have killed the man when he had the chance, or at least thrown him off the Union Pacific train. Walking to Corinne would have taken Haskell a full week.

But there were the businessmen and the hard rock miner with them. Slocum had no idea what they had spoken to Tork Beckwourth about, or why Beckwourth and his partner had gotten into the donnybrook after the well-dressed men left. In some way he couldn't figure right now, that provided the key to the whole puzzle of what had happened at the mine. If only he had been closer and had overheard what they had said.

"John!"

Slocum whipped around in time to grab Polly by the waist. She had stepped into a hole and lost her balance. He swung her around and set her down lightly on firmer ground.

"Thank you. I didn't mean to be a burden, but I wasn't watching where I walked. I'm trying to find where the creature went. Up ahead, I think."

Polly pointed and Slocum knew she thought nothing of her near fall. Her mind was too involved with discovering the monster living in Bear Lake and writing a paper about it.

"Let's set a spell," Slocum suggested. He was tuckered out after all that had happened to him. He groaned as he moved his shoulder. The sudden strain of catching Polly had wrenched his stiff muscles. "I need to wash off some of the blood."

"I'll help," Polly said. Gingerly, she peeled away his shirt. Slocum bit his lower lip as skin came off with the cloth. "Oh, what a mess!"

"Thanks," he said dryly. "I need all the encouragement I can get."

"I didn't mean it like that, John." Polly bent over and lightly kissed his cheek. "I'm not used to seeing such injuries. First Dark Cloud, then you."

"There's a difference. I'm still alive and kicking." He went to the water and began washing off the caked blood on his hands and body. The cold water sharpened his senses. By the time he had finished, Polly had wrung out his shirt. Downright chilly in the soft wind blowing off the lake, the shirt clung to his body like a second skin. Slocum shivered but the cool felt good to him. It reassured him he was still living and alert to anything around him.

"Do you need to rest a little longer?" Polly asked. He saw she worried about his condition.

"I'm fine. I'll be even better when I look that monster square in the eye."

"Good," she said, setting a brisk pace across the uneven terrain, here and there stepping into the water to avoid a dark hole that might cause her to stumble again. Sometimes Slocum led and other times he followed Polly. He found that he became more distracted as he saw her shapely outline and remembered the night they had spent together back in Corinne. Finding the monster became less of a cause for him and simply lying down with the lovely woman grew in importance. Seldom had he found a woman as enticing or exciting as Polly Greene.

"Around here, John. I am sure the creature must have come ashore here. See where the professor stands on the rocky finger sticking into the lake?" She turned and waved to the distant scholar. Slocum couldn't tell if the professor returned the wave, but he saw movement there he interpreted as a reply.

Slocum carefully judged distances and decided she was right. From where they had stood, this would be the most likely spot for a sea monster to come ashore. He bent double and walked slowly along the shore, hunting for any sign the creature had slithered onto land.

"There're some tracks," Slocum said, finding a rocky stretch dappled with mud, "but it doesn't seem big enough for what we saw. Maybe it never comes to land and stays in the lake."

"That's possible, but the professor has other ideas about its species. It ought to come to land to mate and to lair. What else did we find back there?"

Slocum had no answer. But he saw a way he might find one. A mile ahead, up the side of the hill, a dim light shone forth.

"That looks to be a cabin. Settlers along the lake might know something more than we do."

"But can we trust them?" asked Polly. "We have spoken with so many people and Professor Malloy found only one he truly believed. Only Dark Cloud had a consistent story."

"Consistent with what? The professor's idea of what must be here?" Slocum turned skeptical again. He wanted something more than drunken maundering. If anyone had seen the monster, it had to be someone living along the edge of the lake.

Slocum and Polly trudged along, getting to higher ground and then finding a well-trod path leading straight to a cabin. A thick column of smoke curled upward from the chimney and mingling with the pine smoke came the savory odor of stew cooking. That reminded Slocum it had been a coon's age since he had eaten.

"Hello, there. Can we come and talk a spell?"

"Why don't we just go up and—" Polly stopped when Slocum held out his arm, barring her way. She wanted to bull on up to the door. They might do that in Boston, but it wasn't the way settlers greeted strangers.

"Who be ye?" came the question from inside the cabin.

"Name's Slocum. This here is Miss Polly Greene. She's with an expedition come from back East to find out more about the creature living in Bear Lake."

"That all you're after? To see the monster?"

"You've seen it?" cried Polly. "We need to know everything about it. Please. Just a few minutes of your time. Tell me what you can!" The plaintive quality to her entreaty convinced the unseen settler. The cabin door swung open, outlining the man for a moment. Slocum saw a shotgun slung into the crook of the man's arm.

"Come on in. Take care not to let the chickens get you. They're mean."

A rooster lifted its head from under a wing and glared at Slocum. The sight reminded him of his own youth. He had always carried a chicken stick to fend off the more aggressive roosters and hens when he had gone into the yard to feed them. Now he steered Polly around the fowls to the door.

The odor of freshly baked bread turned Slocum weak in the knees. Stew would be fine, but bread cooling amounted to a treat beyond all else to him. His belly growled even as he thrust out his hand in greeting.

"Slocum," the settler said, shaking the hand with a firm grip. "Ye and the lady come on inside. The missus just fixed up dinner. You're welcome to join us."

"We couldn't—" Polly started, but the sight of so much food on the table changed her mind. She stopped inside the door and looked around the cabin, her eyes widening.

Slocum knew what bothered her; he hoped she held her tongue. The settler was a Mormon and they had their own ways. But he had never found more honest or hardworking people.

Two women worked to put the food onto plates and a half dozen children sat at the table, eyes wide at the sight of strangers but obviously hungry and more interested in the food their mothers set out for them.

"Sit down, Miss Greene," Slocum said, guiding Polly toward the table. Two of the children made space for them on the long bench. Slocum waited for the settler to give blessing, then helped himself to the bread and stew. The cup of water with the meal washed down the food. Only when he had taken the edge off his hunger did Slocum ask the questions he needed.

"You have a nice place here, you and your family," Slocum said. "Looks to have been here for quite a few years."

"Four years, since we moved up from Salt Lake City," the man said. "And I know what ye are after."

"Yeah, we saw it. We did," chimed in one of the children. Their father silenced him with a cold look.

"Excuse them. It is seldom we see others and their manners are lacking. We shall attend to that lesson later." The thinly veiled threat silenced the boy.

"Have you seen the creature?"

"No, none of us have," the settler said, choosing his words carefully. Slocum appreciated how meticulous the man was in speech. What would be said would be both succinct and the complete truth. "We have heard strange sounds of late, however."

"How recently?" asked Slocum. It had not occurred to him the monster might be a recent visitor to Bear Lake.

"Within the past six months. At strange times, often during the full moon, we heard the curious bellowing that sounded earlier."

"We heard it. We saw something in the lake, too," Polly rattled on. She had eaten a little of her food, but her enthusiasm pushed aside any hunger. She even forgot her distaste for polygamy and directed her questions toward the two women at the far end of the table. "What of you? Have you seen the creature?"

"No," answered one woman. "Like my husband, I have only heard it late at night. We have no reason to seek it out."

"It poses no danger to us or our children," spoke up the other woman. "If it did, we would be sure to hunt it down."

"I'm sure, but don't you have any curiosity about it? Even if it isn't a threat, surely you want to know what it is, how it lives, where it comes from?" Polly was astounded at their apparent lack of interest in the nocturnal creature swimming around in Bear Lake.

"We have so little time. This is good land, but life is harsh during the winter. We need to devote much time to laying up ample provisions for the winter." The woman turned back to her plate, as if the matter had been resolved.

"I'm sure that is so," said Slocum. "And demands of your religion take up considerable time, also. If you have no direct knowledge, we really ought to go and let you be. Many thanks for the food. It was good." Slocum longingly looked at the heaping bowls still on the table. He could have finished it all himself, but he knew the woman was right. This high in the mountains, winter came quickly and it was vicious. A family without ample food to tide them through the winter was doomed. With so many mouths to feed, the settler had to work especially hard to fill the larder.

"Ye look for answers to questions that don't concern us greatly," the settler said, showing them to the door. "I am sorry we could not be of more help."

"You have helped more than you might think. Again, thank you for the hospitality." Slocum touched the brim of his battered Stetson in the direction of the women, then guided Polly from the cabin.

"Really, John, what have we learned? They might have been lying."

"Why would they do that?" Slocum asked. The notion amused him.

"I don't know. Perhaps they want to keep the discovery for themselves. It will make anyone capturing the creature famous the world over."

"Don't reckon these folks think fame means much. They're hardworking and honest. Nothing they said was a lie. Mormons don't take liquor and don't even cotton much to coffee, tea, or other stimulants. There's nothing to fog their vision or minds."

"Think of the money they could make showing a sea creature in a sideshow."

Slocum was amused at Polly's indignant response. "That something you'd do with the monster, if you catch it?"

"Of course not. This is a scientific matter and not to be made light of." She relaxed and then chuckled. "I see your point. I have reason to want to find the creature. They don't, because it poses no threat to them or their children. But it might."

"If it hasn't in six months, there's not much reason to think it will in the future," Slocum said, his mind racing. "Why did it only appear six months ago? That would be about spring thaw when the ice cleared on the lake."

"The creature might hibernate."

"Something more to discuss with Professor Malloy. It's time to get back to him. Something's got to be done about Dark Cloud's body. It's not civil to let it lay out in the sun, rotting another day."

Polly grimaced at the thought. Together, they made their way back along the lakefront and out to the rocky prominence where Professor Malloy sat, his solitary vigil unrewarded.

"There hasn't been another sound, not a ripple, no trace

at all,'' Malloy bemoaned. Then he yawned widely.

''It's about time we went back to camp. We can spend the night there, then get Dark Cloud's body back to Corinne. If you like, I can leave you two here to watch for the monster.'' Slocum wasn't too happy with this notion. The marshal might take it into his head that Slocum was responsible for the Paiute's death. Talking his way out of jail might prove difficult, but if Malloy gave evidence, the lawman was more likely to believe him.

After all, Professor Hercules Malloy and his lovely assistant were respected scholars, not a drifter with a worn butt on his meticulously maintained six-shooter.

''We need to return to Corinne and retrieve more of our equipment,'' Malloy said. ''I need to take temperature readings in the water, do chemical analyses, all manner of other tests. Yes, we shall definitely accompany you with the body back to Corinne, Mr. Slocum.''

That eased Slocum's mind and seemed to please Polly, also. He caught the gleam in her eye and knew what it meant. They would spend another night in town before returning— and that meant another night together. Slocum had that much more to look forward to when they got to Corinne and finished the unpleasant task of disposing of Dark Cloud's body.

At the top of the hill near where Dark Cloud lay, Slocum cast a last look out at Bear Lake. The quiet waters danced in the moonlight, but no sign of the monster appeared.

''We shall return with the buckboard in the morning for poor Dark Cloud,'' said the professor. He edged around the Paiute's body, then headed for the faint trail along the top of the ridge going back to their camp.

Polly hung back and took Slocum's arm. She said nothing, but laid her head against his shoulder and vented a sigh. He wasn't sure what to make of it, if anything.

''It's a long ways to camp,'' Slocum said. ''Watch your step.''

"I will, John, I will," Polly said. She released her hold and carefully picked her way along behind the professor. Slocum started after her, then paused. In the distance, he heard another mournful bellow of the Bear Lake monster. Or was it only the distant wind?

Slocum hurried along. The answer would be his soon enough.

9

The stench from Dark Cloud's rotting corpse almost gagged Slocum by the time he got the buckboard back to Corinne. He wondered how Professor Malloy and Polly stood the odor. The two of them had spent the entire trip on the hard wooden seat beside him arguing loudly, jotting down notes, and trying to make sense out of their sighting of the monster in the lake. Somehow, their absorption in the project took them away from the foulness drifting up from behind and kept them tightly cocooned in their own academic world.

Slocum envied them all the way to town.

"We ought to go straightaway to the marshal and let him take the body," Slocum said when they reached the small town's city limits.

The professor waved a hand, distracted from the intricate picture he drew in his large notebook. Polly hardly looked up. She cast Slocum a sidelong glance, then returned to point out details the professor had missed in his rendering.

Slocum shook his head. They hadn't seen the creature any better than he had. What they drew in the book was pure nonsense. He wondered how they interpreted the bellowing sound that might have come from some monster lurking under the surface of Bear Lake. A mating call? That notion sent new shivers up and down Slocum's spine. That meant more than one beast swam in those tranquil waters.

"Whoa!" He reined back hard and got the team stopped in front of the town marshal's office. Jumping down, Slocum stretched his aching muscles, then entered the jailhouse. The summer Utah heat vanished and coolness wrapped him up like a blanket. The thick stone walls of the jail held in prisoners and kept out the scorching sunlight. Seated behind his desk, the marshal didn't even notice when Slocum came in.

"I've got some bad news for you, marshal," Slocum said. He was a little uneasy talking to the lawman. He didn't think the marshal had a wanted poster on him lying around, but he could never be sure. It was always best to keep a low profile and let the bullets fly away from him.

"Jist what I need." The marshal kicked back in his chair and hoisted his feet to the edge of his desk. He laced his long fingers behind his head. Stony gaze fixed on Slocum, the marshal dared him to recant the message.

"The Paiute scout, Dark cloud. He's dead."

"Drank himself into a grave, did he now? So?"

"It wasn't like that," Slocum said. "Professor Malloy hired him to do some scouting up at Bear Lake and—"

"The professor?" scoffed the marshal. "He still out there hunting wild gooses?" He chuckled at his little joke. "Never saw a man so set on staring into fog banks and finding monsters. There's nothing in that lake that don't exist in a thousand other places this side of the Rockies."

"Dark Cloud was mauled by something. The professor thinks it was the monster in the lake."

The marshal laughed out loud this time. "And what do you think about Dark Cloud's death? You have the look of a man who's been around, who knows fact from fancy."

"I think you ought to examine the body. Maybe have a doctor study it."

"All Dark Cloud's innards must be pickled by now. No

matter what he done before he came to town, he's been drinkin' himself to death since he showed up a year back.''

"The consumption accounted for that. He needed something to kill the pain,'' said Slocum, wondering why he bristled so at the marshal's words. It slowly came to him he didn't like the lawman's attitude. Whether Dark Cloud had been a hero or a worthless no account, he deserved some respect in death. He certainly deserved having his death investigated because it came under such strange circumstances.

"What consumption? All I ever seen was him scoutin' around for nickels and dimes to go buy more whiskey. Hell.'' The marshal dropped his feet to the floor and stood, hitching up his gun belt. "You say you brought him in? Let me see what I can do.'' The marshal didn't wait for Slocum. He pushed past and went outside into the bright sunlight. He pulled the brim of his hat down to protect his eyes as he went to the rear of the buckboard.

"What a stink!'' he exclaimed. Both Professor Malloy and Polly Greene stared at the lawman. As if they had been drawn back to the world inhabited by everyone else, their noses wrinkled and Polly bit her lower lip, visibly turning ill.

"Go on, take a look,'' Slocum directed. He pulled off the blanket and a cloud of flies flew away. The marshal edged closer and grimaced.

"Seen worse, but not too many,'' he allowed. "Cover the poor bastard up. What do you want from me?''

"An investigation might be in order, marshal,'' suggested Professor Malloy. "He died of some misadventure, to date, inexplicable.''

"Your hired boy here said you thought it was the monster in the lake that did this. You folks don't know about Utah grizzlies. A bear can rip a man's guts out with a single swipe of its paw. Huge, furry brutes. Two swipes could leave a man lookin' like that.'' The marshal backed off another pace.

"I didn't find any trace of a bear," Slocum said. "If a grizzly did this, why not stop and chew on him for a spell? There wasn't anything to drive a bear off once Dark Cloud was dead."

"Who knows what goes on in their thick skulls? Maybe the bear didn't like the way he smelled. Get him on down the street to the undertaker's. Don't reckon the Indian's got any kin to notify. I'm sure as hell he don't have money for a decent funeral. O'Dell can bury him in the potter's field south of town, out there with some of them railroad workers who died of cholera last summer."

"No bear did this, marshal. I want you to form a posse and search for the creature. With a few dozen men, we can flush it out and examine it carefully." Professor Malloy stood as tall as possible but only came to the marshal's chin. His imposing speech did nothing to chip away at the lawman's stony composure.

"With a few dozen men, all askin' a dollar a day, I could round up every desperado in the entire territory. Get movin'. I don't want to tell you again." The marshal had maintained a stolid coolness up to this point. Gagging, the lawman hurried back to his office.

"So much for the idea that he would help us in our hunt. He did not even care that a valiant man lost his life up there," complained Professor Malloy.

"Some folks don't value life too highly. Anyone's life," Slocum said, grabbing the reins. He led the horses down the street. Polly and the professor rode along, then jumped off in front of the funeral parlor. A gloomy man dressed in a long, black broadcloth coat bustled out when he saw he had a customer.

"Dark Cloud," Slocum said simply. "He died."

"Ah, yes, well, there is a small problem," O'Dell started.

"I'll pay for the funeral," spoke up Malloy. "It is the least I can do for such a fine man."

O'Dell blinked, took a second to understand fully what the professor had said, and then smiled broadly. Slocum wished the undertaker hadn't bothered. It reminded him of a grave opening. Quickly making the arrangements, Slocum freed Polly and Malloy of the need to stay at the undertaker's. They returned to the hotel to bathe and rest. Slocum got Dark Cloud's body out of the buckboard and then took the horses to the livery for currying and graining.

He left the stable and looked up and down Corinne's main street. The heat of midday beat down on him, building his thirst. He went to the nearest saloon, a tent pitched so that a breeze blew through to cool off the customers as they drank. The bar was nothing more than a rough plank dropped onto sawhorses, but there was nothing wrong with the liquor the barkeep poured. Slocum drank the first shot with real appreciation. Some of his aches and pains faded and he knew, a little, what Dark Cloud had seen in the fiery whiskey.

Sipping more slowly at a second drink, Slocum turned so the hot wind blew over his face to cool him even more. His eyes widened when he saw the two businessmen from the mine. They huddled together at the rear of the tent, ardently discussing something. One smashed his hand down on the tottering table, spilling his drink. The other hardly noticed.

"Barkeep," Slocum called. "Send two more drinks to those gents." He pointed to the businessmen.

"You know them?" The barkeep's brow furrowed.

"Seems like I've met them somewhere," Slocum said slowly. "Can't rightly remember where, though. You know their names?"

"They blowed into Corinne like some tornado of greenbacks. They're from out in San Francisco. That's 'bout all I know of 'em."

Slocum nodded. The barkeep took the drinks over and pointed Slocum out as their benefactor. Neither man seemed inclined to thank Slocum for his generosity, so Slocum walked over.

"Afternoon," he said, studying them up close. He had thought them prosperous from his brief glimpse through a knothole in Beckwourth's powder shed. Now he realized they were more than simply wealthy. The diamond headlights they wore had to weigh out at two carats or better. Silk suits, fancy cufflinks of gold and rubies, shoes that had once been highly polished and now carried a thin film of Utah dust, all told of huge fortunes. Slocum had seen Leland Stanford once and the railroad magnate hadn't been this lavishly attired.

"Who are you?" No hint of civility. Slocum decided he didn't matter because he wasn't of their social class.

"Saw you out at Beckwourth and Lawton's mine yesterday. Mind if I ask what your interest is?"

The men jumped as if they had been stuck. They exchanged a quick look. The larger of the men spoke carefully. "We represent a consortium interested in purchasing select mining properties. You don't have the look of a miner, but maybe you know of a producing mine or two we might buy."

"Can't say that I do," Slocum allowed. "You thinking on buying the Beckwourth-Lawton mine?"

"Our business is private, sir," the smaller of the pair said stiffly. The way he turned around shut Slocum off from any further talk. Slocum backed off and left the saloon without another word to them. But as he stepped into the street, his mind raced. They had been interested in buying the mine the two miners had touted as being the richest this side of Battle Mountain.

Slocum had been inside the mine and knew it had never produced the nugget Tork Beckwourth flashed around town. And the traces of gold he had seen in the rock might have been put there—salted.

Beginning a circuit of all the saloons in Corinne, Slocum had to look in only four until he found the hard rock miner who had accompanied the two San Francisco businessmen.

He went to the bar and stood next to the man, ordering another whiskey. Slocum was feeling a mite lightheaded from the earlier whiskey, but it still went down smooth as silk. He let out a loud sigh of relief as he finished the drink.

"That really takes care of my thirst. I swear, being out in the sun is like having a desert stuck in your throat." The miner nodded slightly, nursing his own drink. "You from Corinne?" Slocum asked. "I've been looking for mining property and just got into town."

"You?" The miner reared back and studied Slocum from head to toe. "You don't look as if you've got two nickels to rub together."

Slocum smiled. "I don't, but my principals do. A group from New Orleans. Rich bastards."

"What is it about this miserable place?" grumbled the miner.

"How's that?" Slocum knew he had primed the pump. He needed only to wait for the gush of information to spew forth.

"A couple big-shot tycoons from San Francisco hired me to scout out mines for them," the miner said. "I told them there wasn't much to buy around here, but they were eager to waste their money."

"I heard tell of a big strike north of town, out near Bear Lake," Slocum said. "A big fellow, Tork Beckwourth by name. He flashed a huge nugget the size of your fist. I heard about it."

The miner snorted in disgust, finishing his drink. He ordered another. "I saw the nugget. Where that galoot got it, I don't know, but it didn't come from his hole out by the lake. That mine is well nigh worthless."

"Do tell. I read up on the claim over at the assay office. Looked good to me."

"The assay is wrong," the miner said flatly. "Has to be. Or maybe the chemist's kid did the work. I saw him out back doing some of his old man's assaying. Whatever happened, that mine is an empty hole. Hell, they didn't even dig it out. They followed a natural vent back into the hillside."

"No gold at all?" Slocum kept from smiling.

"Danged little. You'd do well to find other mines, and I'm not just sayin' that to run you off. Hell, I don't want to scout any more mines for those two dudes. For all their expensive clothes and flashy ways, they don't pay squat."

Slocum laughed. "Same with the fellows from Saint Louis."

"Saint Louis? I thought you said you worked for somebody in New Orleans." The miner turned a gimlet eye on Slocum.

"Big company," Slocum lied. "The main office is down in New Orleans, but the guy who hired me is from Saint Louis."

"Hmm." The miner worked some more on his drink. Slocum considered moving on, but he had to know more.

"Would those miners dynamite their own claim?"

"Why'd you ask that? Hell, they're tryin' to foist it off on somebody who doesn't know his ore. If the shaft collapsed, they'd have no chance to sell that glory hole. Nobody'd believe that nugget came from a closed mine and Beckwourth and Lawton didn't want to reopen it."

Slocum conceded the miner had a point. Tork Beckwourth had to convince people of the value of the mine and couldn't do that if he let the collapse stand. He and Gold Tooth Lawton had to be seen working hard to reopen the shaft, if they wanted to sell the mine.

So who had tossed the dynamite into the mine to trap Slocum? Haskell? Slocum still didn't know what Haskell's part was in the fraud the two Bear Lake miners were trying to run.

"If I come across anything, I'll let you know," Slocum said.

"Don't bother. Them gents are plannin' on blowin' town when the next train chugs through. Don't know if I'll be goin' with them. Probably so. Even though they don't pay too good, it beats haulin' ten tons of ore from a pit every shift."

Slocum finished his drink and left the saloon. The liquor had turned him tipsy. He saw a barbershop across the street. A shave and bath would do him a world of good, then a good meal to top it off. By that time, Polly would have rested up and finished with her arguments over the Bear Lake monster. Maybe the two of them could spend some time together.

Whistling, Slocum crossed the street to the barbershop. As he started to enter, he heard a low voice. "Come on over here. You want to know about Beckwourth and Lawton's mine?"

"Who's there?" He looked around and decided the hidden man had to be in the narrow alleyway beside the barbershop. Slocum walked over, wary of entering.

From the far end of the alley, a shot rang out. Slocum felt a searing pain in his head. Then blackness closed around him and he fell to the ground.

10

Darkness turned to dazzling brilliance. Slocum rolled to his side and the light went away, but his face rubbed over dirt. He spat out a mouthful of grit, then pushed himself to his hands and knees. His head buzzed as if a nest of hornets had taken up residence. Slocum's strength faded suddenly and he fell back to the ground—and this weakness saved him from taking a second bullet.

The lead whizzed through the air and splatted into the street a few feet beyond him.

The nearness of the bushwhacker's second shot filled Slocum with red fury. He rolled hard, his hand going for his Colt Navy. He drew and cocked the six-shooter and fired, not caring if he had anyone in his sights. He had to drive away the sidewinder trying to dry-gulch him—long enough to recover, Slocum hoped.

His bullet whined down the alleyway and produced a frightened yelp. Slocum sat up. His vision blurred. Blood trickled from the crease at the side of his skull, but he ignored the pain. Blinking hard, he got a better look at the man still crouching down the alley.

"Wallings!" he cried, recognizing the man from Ben's Drink Emporium who had bragged about seeing the Bear

Lake monster. The miner took off like a frightened deer.
Slocum got off a second shot, cursing when he missed by a
country mile. He forced himself to his feet and staggered a
few paces. Slocum had to lean against the barbershop wall
to regain his senses. He pushed his Stetson back and used
his bandanna to dab at the sluggish flow of blood. Tying the
red cloth around the wound before pulling his hat back down,
Slocum knew he looked like something the cat had dragged
in, and he didn't much care.

For whatever reason, Ash Wallings had tried to kill him,
and the man wasn't going to get away with it. Since coming
to Corinne, Slocum had been tied up, blown up in a mine,
and now dry-gulched. Dark Cloud had been killed, and Slocum intended to add Wallings to the list of the dead.

Slocum got to the end of the alley, took a deep breath,
then swung around as he went into a crouch. His six-shooter
centered on . . . nothing. Cursing, Slocum took off after the
fleeing back-shooter, hearing the pounding of heavy feet
ahead. He skidded to a halt when he came to the corner of
the town's general store. Again he swung around, crouched
and ready to fire. This time he found a target.

Wallings stood in the center of the street, frantically
searching for a way out.

"Wallings!" Slocum shouted. He wanted Wallings's hide
but wasn't going to shoot the man in the back. Slocum was
better than that. That would look too much like murder. Besides, he wanted to see the man's face as he died. The miner
turned, his rifle in his hands.

"Slocum!" Wallings started firing, levering one shell after
another into the chamber and pulling the trigger as fast as
he could. Slocum took aim carefully and fired. Wallings staggered and sat down in the street.

Stupidly, Wallings stared at his hands. Slocum rose and
sighted down the barrel of his Colt again. He cocked his gun
deliberately and squeezed off another round. This one hit

Wallings in the shoulder and spun him around to lie face-down in the middle of the street. Slocum walked slowly to stand in the mouth of the alley, waiting to make sure he had killed Wallings.

The miner groaned and moved. Bringing up his pistol, Slocum prepared to finish him off.

He never saw Elias Kenyon approaching. Wallings's partner dropped one shoulder, charged forward, and hit Slocum hard just below the hips. Slocum's shot went wild, sailing off to frighten a few sea gulls flying overhead. Staggering, Slocum fought to keep his balance. Kenyon kept driving, his legs pumping hard.

Slocum slammed into a post holding up a porch overhang and knocked it down. Shingles and wood splinters cascaded around him as he kicked and fought to get away from Kenyon. He succeeded in planting his boot in the man's face, but the blow wasn't enough to stop Kenyon.

He held off triggering another round until he could get free of the debris encumbering him. He scooted away until he got out from under the fallen roofing, then saw Elias Kenyon helping his wounded partner across the street. Slocum fired again, missed, and the next time the hammer fell on an empty cylinder.

Jamming his six-shooter into his holster, Slocum took off after the fleeing men. He didn't know why Wallings had tried to murder him, but he was going to find out. Elias Kenyon might have only been defending his partner, but Slocum didn't think so.

Slocum ignored the people timidly poking their heads out to see what the fuss was all about. He bent low and scooped up Wallings's fallen rifle. The bullet intended to end the miner's life had ricocheted off the side of the rifle, ruining the mechanism. That might have saved Slocum from dodging another shot, but he wished he had been a fraction of an inch to one side. That would have finished Wallings.

"Where did you go?" Slocum bellowed. He hunted for Wallings and his partner but didn't see them anywhere. He took a deep breath and settled down. He was still furious, but his heated emotions cooled. Slocum wanted the men, but his reason took over. Walking along the next street over, Slocum's keen eyes sought any trace of blood in the dry dust. He found one. He bent and put his finger to the dark brown lump on the ground.

"Fresh," he decided. Slocum picked up the pace and was soon running. The spots of blood came more frequently. Wallings bled profusely from the one good shot Slocum had made. Not wanting to take time to reload, Slocum vowed to take on both men with his bare hands. He was up to it. Cold fury drove him.

"Stop!" he shouted when he spotted them down the street. Wallings slumped forward over the neck of his horse. Elias Kenyon had somehow gotten his larger partner onto a horse. Kenyon jumped into the saddle of his own mount and put his heels to its flanks. The horse jumped as if stuck on the rump with a branding iron. Wallings's horse followed. Slocum chased them a few yards, then knew he could never overtake the pair. They had gotten away.

He considered going to the livery and getting his gray gelding, then discarded that notion. The time it would take to get the saddle horse from the livery would give Wallings and Kenyon plenty of time to vanish down the road and into the mountains. Slocum wasn't up to doing any tracking at the moment.

"What's goin' on?" came the marshal's querulous voice from behind Slocum.

He turned and stared at the lawman. "Nothing, marshal. Nothing at all." Slocum walked away, fuming at his inability to stop either of the miners. He had been through too much and sorely wanted some rest, a bath, and a meal.

He also wanted revenge—especially revenge.

*   *   *

Professor Hercules Malloy glanced up from the writing desk in the hotel lobby. One eyebrow arched when he noticed Slocum's condition. The scholar pushed back slightly from the table, letting Slocum see the intricate pictures he drew of the monster in the lake.

"Really, sir, you should be more careful. I do not appreciate men in my employ who carouse." The professor sniffed and turned back to his work, doodling numbers along the margin of a page already filled with crabbed writing. Slocum had no idea what it meant, and right now, he didn't much care. Let the professor think he had been out drinking and fighting in some saloon.

One step at a time, he went up the stairs, not sure if it was his body or the stairs creaking so. He reached the top and stopped. He wasn't thinking too clearly. Polly and the professor had returned to the hotel, but they had checked out days before. That meant they had new rooms—and Slocum hadn't registered for a new one. He would have to go back, find the desk clerk, and get a room if he wanted to stretch out and let his body recover.

Turning, he started back down when he heard a stifled gasp. He swung about to see Polly standing in the doorway of the room she had occupied before.

"John, you're a mess!"

"Thanks for the compliment," he said. "You should see the other two." Slocum's fists clenched, thinking of Wallings and Kenyon. Ash Wallings might be carrying one of Slocum's slugs in his body, but Elias Kenyon had escaped without even a scratch.

As Slocum considered what he might do to the two low-down, treacherous back-shooters, his anger tempered with growing curiosity. Why had Wallings tried to kill him? He hardly knew the man. They had been in a saloon together while Tork Beckwourth was bragging about his nugget pulled from his mine. Wallings had been telling anyone who would listen that he had seen the Bear Lake monster.

Slocum shook his head and immediately regretted it. A wave of dizziness swept over him. He grabbed for the wall to support himself and almost fell.

"John, come in. Hurry. You cannot even stand without wobbling." Strong hands guided him into the room. Slocum wasn't quite sure for a moment who was leading him. Then his vision cleared and he saw Polly Greene.

"Thanks," he said, meaning it. He sank down on the bed. "Reckon I got bunged up more than I thought."

"You've been shot!" Polly touched the crease along the side of his skull and Slocum thought his head would explode. He pulled away. She took his head firmly in her hands and drew him closer. Slocum found himself lacking any strength to resist.

He pressed his face into her breasts, weakness assailing him again. Slocum let the woman work on the bullet crease, gently dabbing it with his bandanna dipped in water from a basin on her dresser. Polly didn't stop there. She worked to clean the rest of his face.

"You look halfway respectable," she said, studying her handiwork. "The wound wasn't as serious as it looked. It must have bled forever, though. What happened?"

Slocum quickly told her. Polly turned pale when he mentioned tracking down Ash Wallings and trying to kill him.

"Things are done differently back at Harvard," she said in a small voice. "The police would take care of a man like this Ash Wallings." She swallowed hard. "That is, if such a shoot-out ever happened in Cambridge. I don't recollect one the entire time I've attended university."

"This is the West," Slocum said. "Out here we don't take the time to find the law if we can set things right ourselves."

"Look what happened to you," she said, sitting beside him.

"He shot me before I even knew who he was," Slocum pointed out. "Nothing much came my way after I found him out."

"He tried to murder you, for no reason."

"For no reason." The words rang hollow in Slocum's ear. Nobody went off the handle and tried to gun down another man. Even if Ash Wallings had been liquored up, he wouldn't have tried killing Slocum the way he had. Slocum had no objection to a man wanting to get drunk and let off a little steam. A good fistfight now and then kept him alert. But he had heard of few men who got drunk and then laid in wait to shoot whoever walked by.

Wallings had recognized him and had *then* tried to kill him, John Slocum. Why?

"Lie back on the bed. Rest, John. You need to sleep."

"I'm too filthy to muss up your bed," Slocum said. He tried to sit up, but Polly firmly held him down.

"You'd never be too filthy for anything, John. For anything at all." She hovered above him like an angel. Her blond hair caught sunlight coming through the window. The strands dangling down across her face turned to spun gold. Her gray eyes looked down on him and saw—what? Slocum was at a loss to tell. She was well-to-do, a scholar, and obviously expert at what she did. Otherwise, the usually oblivious Professor Malloy would never had brought her halfway across the continent.

"You are so different from anyone I have ever known. The others, the ones at school, are all so . . ." Words escaped her.

Slocum knew how to finish the sentence. And it wasn't with words. He drew her down and lightly kissed her lips. If she didn't mind that he smelled like a pig in slop, he wasn't going to argue with her. Not a woman this lovely.

The kiss deepened. Her tongue darted out and tangled with his. Back and forth their tongues raced, duelling erotically, mouths entrapping each other for a moment, then letting go. Polly began breathing more heavily as her passion mounted.

Her fingers worked on Slocum's grimy clothing, tugging and moving, getting his shirt off him. Slocum helped by discarding his gun belt and boots. Polly sat back and watched as he unbuttoned his jeans.

"Let me," she said, her breasts rising and falling even more. Bending over, she ran her fingers along the waistband and then dipped them down inside. Slocum gasped as she touched the side of his growing manhood. He hardened as Polly began stroking, teasing, drawing her fingernails along the edge in a way that made him both weak and strong at the same time.

"Can't let you do that much longer," Slocum said. Polly slid his trousers down and exposed his crotch. His member was standing upright like a flagpole in the middle of a cavalry outpost. The blond circled her fingers and began running her hand up and down in a motion Slocum found undeniably exciting. Too exciting.

"Then I'll stop," she said, sitting back primly on the bed. But the expression on her seductive face belied her words. "What do you prefer to do?"

"This," Slocum said, reaching over and tugging at the ties on her blouse. Then he worked on the buttons, clumsily popping one after another free. Polly stood and stepped away from him, but Slocum was too quick. His nimble fingers had unfastened her skirt before she stood. The cloth slithered down over her flaring hips to reveal long, slender legs. The sight was almost as exciting to him as what Polly had been doing at his groin.

"Turn around," he said. "Let me see you from all sides."

Polly obeyed, turning slowly, arms lifted. Every time she turned, Slocum got off another piece of her underclothing. When she stood entirely naked in the warm sunlight coming through the window, he knew he could stand the tensions mounting in his loins no longer.

He lunged for Polly and pulled her toward him. She melted into his arms. They fit together perfectly. Rolling onto the bed, Slocum felt her legs open willingly for him. He moved, his hips in position above her. For a moment, he looked down into her face.

Polly's eyes were closed and her mouth slightly open. She moaned constantly with the desire building within her. The eyelids opened partially and she said, "Now, John. I want you now."

He slid forward, his manhood buried fully within her softly yielding body. A shudder passed through Polly and communicated itself to Slocum. The strong twitches of the tight female flesh around him made him think of milking a cow. He tried to pull out, but she held him too firmly. Straining, Polly arched her back and ground herself into his crotch.

Slocum trembled with need. He levered back until he was only partially within her, the woman's nether lips wetly kissing his length. Then he dipped forward, again taking both their breaths away. Buried balls deep, he rotated his hips, stirring her and himself. Over and over he moved, kissing, stroking, lightly nibbling at her nipples, doing all he could to drive her wild with passion.

He succeeded.

Polly shook all over, her body raging like a turbulent sea. She clawed at his back even as she lifted up and tried to take even more of him into her body.

"Yes, oh, yes, yes," she moaned out. Polly gave a final shudder and subsided as Slocum lost control. The fierce surge from his loins shot into her, setting off a second, lesser shiver of delight.

Spent, Slocum slumped down, arms still around Polly. She turned over and dreamily clung to him, her head nestled in the hollow of his shoulder. For a few minutes, they simply lay together. Then Polly moved away enough so she could look up into his face. Her eyes glowed. Never had he seen a woman so radiant. Polly obviously expected him to speak. Slocum wasn't sure what to say. Seldom in his life had he felt this way, and words refused to come easily.

"John?" Polly asked in a whisper. "How long?"

"How long for what?" he asked.

"How long before we find the creature in the lake? I don't want to return to Harvard. I don't want to leave you."

He started to tell her she didn't have to go, monster or no. Then he simply said, "I don't know."

And he didn't.

11

Slocum and Polly Greene lay side by side a short while longer, then she slipped from his arms and sat up. She heaved a deep sigh. Slocum had no idea what thoughts ran through her mind since he couldn't see her face. She bent over and grabbed her discarded clothing. Deliberately, Polly began dressing.

"I should never have said anything like that, John."

"Like what?" But Slocum knew what she meant. What had passed between them was unique, and she had broken the bubblelike magic spell by pointing out that they came from different worlds. When she and Professor Malloy finished their hunt for whatever lived in the lake, she would return East and he would go on his way.

Slocum had no idea where he would go. Just somewhere else. That made them different, his freedom and her lack of it.

"Have you seen the pen-and-ink drawing the professor made of the creature?" Polly asked. "It is quite representative of what we believe the beast looks like."

"You said you never saw it, no more than I did, at any rate," Slocum pointed out.

"True, but we believe it belongs to a special group of

reptiles. It can move about on the land but prefers the water. We are quite familiar with this particular breed, though of course, they are much smaller than the one living in Bear Lake.''

''The lair is where it sleeps?'' Slocum asked, not sure if he believed it. Alligators down in the Louisiana bayous spent most of their time in the water. He wasn't sure if they had any kind of lair, at least none that he had ever heard about.

''Not in the sense that birds have nests,'' Polly said, fastening the last button on her blouse. She smoothed out nonexistent wrinkles and went to the window, looking into the street. Slocum took this as a signal for him to get dressed. He started moving, aware of the aches in his body. ''However, there might be a lair where the creature mates.''

Slocum held back his comparison of this room to the fetid lair they had found on the rocky peninsula jutting out into the lake. He pulled on his boots, then cinched down his cross-draw holster until it felt just right.

''It lays eggs? Heard tell that's what a gator does.'' He kept comparing the monster in the water with an alligator, though there was little similarity if the towering mounds of flesh he had seen were real. An alligator didn't rear up out of the water, trailing behind a loop or two of body like some impossible reptilian freight train. They kept low in the water and were sometimes mistaken for floating logs.

But he remembered the crunch and gritting under his boots when moving around in the lair. There had not been enough light to see, but it had reminded him of eggshell as he broke it.

''We believe that is the case,'' Polly said, turning back. He couldn't tell if she were relieved that he had dressed. Settling into the chair by the window, she divided her time between him and the torpid movement of Corinne's citizens as they moved about in the late-afternoon heat. ''We ought to have examined the lair more carefully, but there was so much happening."

"Dark Cloud dying," Slocum said. But he only listened with half an ear to Polly's theories about the creature.

The Paiute's death was another of the curious imponderables that had happened since he had signed on with Professor Malloy. What had killed Dark Cloud? Slocum had seen men mauled by bears. The Indian's body was badly mutilated, but no bear had ripped him apart. Any grizzly worth its salt would have bitten down hard on the Paiute's neck to keep him from running, then used its claws to gut him. Slocum had seen no wounds save for those on the man's belly.

Dark Cloud. Ash Wallings. And Tork Beckwourth's attempt to get rid of Slocum. Had the miner wanted to do more than simply hog-tie him? Slocum had every reason to think Beckwourth and his partner had tried to kill him to keep him from jinxing their sale of the mine to the San Francisco businessmen. But it made no sense that they would dynamite their own property. They would never be able to sell the hole in the ground if they turned it into a rubble-filled mine.

Nobody buying a gold mine wanted to go to the effort of reopening the pit, even if a fabulous mother lode lay below. From all the businessmen's mining expert had said, Beckwourth and Lawton's mine was as close to useless as tits on a bull.

Slocum got up and went to the window to see what interested Polly so. He couldn't tell. The few people daring the heat went about their business without any fuss or fanfare.

"It is so different from Boston," she said, looking past him into the dusty street. She heaved a deep, soulful breath. "How do you ever get used to the primitive conditions?"

"Don't much notice them," Slocum said.

"You are such a stoic," sighed Polly. She had misinterpreted what he meant. To Slocum, life in Corinne was no different from life anywhere else. The only big difference lay in the availability of liquor. With thirteen saloons left over from the railroad construction, he could slake his thirst anywhere along the street. Unless he had a bottle with him, that was something he couldn't do out on the trail or even a few miles to the south in Salt Lake City. The Mormons considered drinking an evil, not only among their own kind but for everyone else. That was a big reason Slocum didn't do much more than pass through Utah on his way to other places.

He stiffened and moved closer to the window when he saw a familiar face across the street.

"What is it, John?" Polly noticed his immediate interest in an otherwise ordinary parade of citizens.

"Joe Haskell, the tinhorn gambler from the train," he said. "Wonder what that cayuse is up to now?"

Haskell walked beside a man hidden by the overhang of a store. The two stopped, Haskell's jaw flapping in the wind. Slocum wondered if the man would ever shut up, even to take a breath. He gestured wildly and talked a blue streak. Then the man with him moved into view. Slocum nodded slowly, understanding what was going on. Haskell was trying to sell Beckwourth and Lawton's mine to another sucker.

"What are you going to do, John? Didn't you say he was the one who trapped you in the mine?"

Slocum started to confirm that, then bit back the words. "I'm not sure. These days, I'm not sure of much of anything." He looked at Polly and knew his uncertainty ran deeper than anything the gambler Haskell might be doing— or any of the miners running loose in the Bear Lake area.

"Go on," she said. "I see you getting all anxious. Champing at the bit, I heard someone say."

Slocum had to smile at this. He bent and kissed her lightly, then left before anything more could be said. Slocum wasn't used to feeling what he did for Polly Greene. A woman like her deserved more than he could ever offer. Professor Malloy belonged in her world, not John Slocum.

Slocum saw the professor still worked diligently at his drawing of the monster he had barely seen. Not stopping, Slocum went outside into the heat. He felt as if he had walked into a furnace. Summer increasingly wore down on the land, in spite of Corinne being at the edge of the Utah desert. He wished they were back up in the mountains at Bear Lake, and it didn't much matter if they were hunting for a monster living there. It was cooler, and Slocum had to admit that the extended Mormon family they had talked with might have the right idea. Life could be harsh in the winter, but the summers were decent and the land might give a man enough to live off.

He shook off the way his thoughts turned and started across the street to find Joe Haskell. The gambler and his mark had vanished, but Slocum was sure he could find them easily enough.

"Damnation," he muttered under his breath when he saw Haskell riding out of town as fast as his horse could take him. Slocum considered whether following the gambler or finding the businessman gave him the best chance for garnering a tad more information.

Somehow, Joe Haskell was mixed up in the problems he was having, but Polly was right on one point. He couldn't accuse Haskell of dynamiting the mine without more evidence. To cut down the gambler and leave the real culprit free didn't set well with Slocum, not that Joe Haskell wasn't guilty of enough on his own.

"Hey, hold up!" Slocum called when he saw the businessman walking from the assay office. He hurried over to the man who studied him like a bug crawling across his nose.

"What is it?" the man said in a surly voice.

"You and Joe Haskell. He trying to sell you the mine up at Bear Lake?"

"What of it?"

"I'm interested in the same mine," Slocum lied. "I represent some buyers from New Orleans." He saw no reason not to repeat the lie he had told the others Haskell had brought to the mine. "I've checked the output and didn't think much of it. I was wondering what your opinion was."

"My opinions are my own. If I choose to purchase the mine, I shall, but I will not be bullied into a bidding war for it." The man spun and stalked off, leaving Slocum even more confused. This didn't sound like a man hot to buy a valuable property. If anything, his anger carried more than his determination. Haskell might have inveigled the businessman out to the mine to see it firsthand, but it seemed his mark had already refused to go with him.

"The mine," Slocum said to himself. "That's where the answers are." He went to the livery and saddled his gray. The horse snorted when it saw him, not wanting to put up with Slocum's weight again. Slocum had driven the buckboard back, letting the horse trail behind. But the animal settled down when Slocum swung into the saddle. He patted the horse's neck, then headed for Bear Lake at a trot, intending to find Haskell as quickly as possible.

Slocum approached cautiously. He rode up the road leading to Beckwourth and Lawton's mine, noting the recent spoor. A fresh pile of manure told him Haskell had come by not twenty minutes ahead. Slocum would have made better time if he hadn't missed the path leading off the road. The miners hadn't bothered marking their property, and he had backtracked before finding the proper course.

Slipping from the saddle, Slocum tethered his gray and advanced on foot. His hand flashed to his Colt Navy when a gunshot echoed down the mountain. Going into a crouch, Slocum hurried forward to find a place to spy on the mine and the miners.

Of Tork Beckwourth and Gold Tooth Lawton he saw no

trace. They seemed to have left the mine and not returned. But Haskell's horse stood by the run-down cabin. Of the gambler Slocum saw no trace, either. But a second blast came.

Cocking his six-shooter, Slocum hurried forward and used the cabin to shield him from probing eyes. Edging along, Slocum chanced a quick look around the corner. For a moment, he wasn't sure what Joe Haskell was doing at the mouth of the mine. Some work had been done to clear the fall caused by the dynamite. Slocum wondered if his sudden appearance would startle Haskell. Did the gambler think Slocum's body was buried under tons of rock?

Slocum started to reveal himself to see Haskell's reaction when the gambler lifted a shotgun and fired it. Slocum dropped facedown, thinking Haskell had fired at him. But the sounds following the report told Slocum something more than attack was being done. Lifting to his elbows, Slocum saw Haskell ramming something into the barrels of the shotgun he had just discharged.

"Salting," Slocum said. "The son of a bitch is salting the mine. He wants to sell it by showing off the gold he's blasting into the rock."

Haskell fired several more loads into the rock just inside the mouth. Slocum inched back and sat behind the cabin, waiting for Haskell to finish. If he showed himself to Haskell—and if Haskell had been responsible for trying to bury him alive—all Slocum could do was shoot the owlhoot where he stood. Too many questions would go unanswered if he did that. Better to learn as much as he could before showing himself to the gambler.

Slocum might even uncover Haskell's connection with Beckwourth and Lawton, though that was increasingly obvious. The miners wanted to unload a worthless mine and had been talked into letting Haskell sell it for them, probably after taking a huge cut. The more Joe Haskell got for the hole in the ground, the more he rode out with in his pocket.

Making his way back to his horse, Slocum thought this might be the reason Haskell had tried to silence Ash Wallings and Elias Kenyon about the monster in the lake. Bear Lake lay over the hill, not that distant. Rumors of a monster coming out of the water to eat people would drive off potential buyers.

Slocum's thoughts turned back to Dark Cloud. Something had killed the Paiute. It didn't seem likely it was Haskell or the two miners. The marshal had been willing to discount the death as accidental, caused by a grizzly. Slocum didn't think any bear had done the killing, and he sure as hell didn't believe a reptile had slithered out of Bear Lake to do the killing.

That left two-legged varmints. But why kill the Indian? It made no sense. Certainly it made no sense for Haskell to be salting this mine. Some work had been done to clean out the debris, but not much. The main plug of rock that had trapped Slocum still stretched for several yards into the mine, making any gold taking unlikely. But the rock around the mouth would gleam brightly from Haskell's salting.

"Stupid son of a bitch. Nobody's going to believe gold out in plain sight like that." Haskell couldn't even salt a mine without arousing suspicion. Turning his horse, Slocum started back to Corinne, letting the gray choose its own pace. He saw no reason to hurry, and he needed time to think over the puzzles coming down around him like hailstones.

Slocum dismounted and tethered his horse in front of the assay office. He wanted to find out what the initial survey on the mine might be. Inside the assay office, he saw two men working diligently with their chemicals and small kilns to get the pay dirt from samples.

"Howdy," greeted one man, using tongs to pull his crucible from a kiln. "How can I help you?"

"Need to know about a mine."

"You, too?" The assayer grumbled to himself. "Don't reckon you're thinking about the Lovely Lady Mine?"

"The one Joe Haskell is trying to sell for Beckwourth and Lawton?"

"That's the one. Go on, do your lookin'. The book's on my desk." He pointed at a small pine board nailed to the wall. "It'll fall open to the right page, so many's been lookin' the past day or two."

"Tell me about the Lovely Lady," Slocum suggested.

"Not much to say. It isn't the best mine in Utah. Not the worst, either. It takes a powerful lot of work to make any mine reporting two ounces of gold per ton to work. So, the ore is there, but it's not worth all the attention it's been gettin'."

"No reason to salt the mine?"

"Hell, there's always reason to do that to high-grade the ore. Makes the property seem better 'n it is. But you're not accusin' anybody of that, are you?"

"The property in Beckwourth's and Lawton's names?"

"All legal and proper. They been diggin' out there well nigh two years now. They make enough to live on but not much more. Heard they're gettin' itchy feet and want to move on."

"Think it might be played out?"

"You'll have to ask the owners. I can't make comment on such things. Bring me ore, I'll tell you what it's worth. Other than that . . ." The assayer shrugged and turned back to his work.

Slocum left the office and stood outside, seeing that it was almost sundown. He pushed back his Stetson and wiped sweat from his face. He winced as he touched the crease on the side of his head. That reminded him of Wallings and how the man had tried to bushwhack him.

Rubbing his belly, he remembered he was a few meals shy

of three for the day. He had ridden hard and not had the time to eat. Slocum turned to go to the hotel. If Polly wanted to join him, they could have dinner at the café down the street.

Slocum started across the street when he heard a six-gun cock behind him. He started for his six-shooter but was frozen when he heard the cold command, "Reach for that piece of iron and you're dead, Slocum."

Slocum turned slowly, hands away from his pistol. He faced the Corinne marshal.

"What's wrong, marshal?" he asked, aware of the size of the lawman's six-shooter pointed at him. The bore looked big enough to run a train down.

"You're under arrest, Slocum. For the murder of Joe Haskell."

12

"What the blue blazes are you talking about, marshal?" If the man had said rocks fell from the sky, Slocum couldn't have been more surprised. "I haven't killed anyone. Why, I just saw Haskell not three hours back. He—"

"He was out at the Lovely Lady. You shot the poor son of a buck in the back, Slocum. We got you fair and square on this," the marshal said, his six-shooter not wavering.

Slocum didn't know how to react to the outrageous charge. He had seen Haskell alive. He knew he could never draw down on the marshal and live longer than it took for a bullet to rip out his heart. His mouth opened, but no words came out.

"Lift that fancy six-shooter of yours out. Use your left hand!" The marshal shoved his pistol in the direction of Slocum's face. The bore looked even bigger now than it had when Slocum had first peered down at it.

Slocum did as he was told. The marshal circled warily, picked up the ebony handled six-gun, and tucked it into his belt. He waved his gun in the direction of the jailhouse. Slocum walked slowly, considering his chances. They didn't look good. This time, when he entered the marshal's cool office from the hot street, it no longer seemed refreshing. Slocum shuddered.

"Into the back. We got the cage a-waitin' for you, Slocum." The marshal poked him in the back with his gun and steered Slocum to the empty cell at the rear. A quick glance told Slocum he had no chance of breaking out. Corinne didn't use a room in an adobe hut like so many places in the Southwest. He entered a real cage with iron straps on all sides, floor, ceiling, and all four walls. To pop the rivets holding the straps together would take hours of hard work using a pry bar—which Slocum wasn't likely to get.

The sound of the iron doors locking behind him carried such finality to it, Slocum wondered if he would ever see the light of day again.

"Tell me what evidence you have, marshal," Slocum called at the lawman's back. The marshal laughed harshly. The sound of the door leading to his office slamming shut was all the answer Slocum got. He sank down to the hard bunk, wondering what was going on.

"What you in for, mister?" called a prisoner in the other cell. "They got me for drunk 'n' disorderly."

Slocum glanced in the man's direction and decided the drunk was better off in jail than out. He didn't look to have eaten a square meal in a long, long time.

"They think I killed a tinhorn gambler," Slocum said. "You know anything about it?"

"Well, I been listenin' hard and my cell's real near the office door," the man said, jerking his thumb in the direction of the marshal's office. "You aren't talkin' about Joe Haskell, now, are you?"

"Yeah," Slocum said. "What did you hear?"

"They think you bushwhacked him out at the Lovely Lady a couple hours back," the man said, relishing the telling. "Seems some gent he was tryin' to sell the mine to showed up and found Haskell dead as a doornail."

"So why do they think I did it?"

"From what was bein' said to the marshal, who else in

Corinne is likely to want Haskell dead? They said you had a run-in with him on the train before you arrived, there was somethin' about you and him havin' a shoot-out yesterday. Bad blood. That's the reason they're gonna drop a noose around your neck.''

"There's no need for you to sound so happy about it," Slocum growled. He paced the tiny cage like a tiger, then sat down and thought hard. He had to get out. He had been in more secure jails in his day—and had gotten free without benefit of the law releasing him. But he usually had a partner outside willing to risk a few bullets for him.

Slocum began going over the cage rivet by rivet, much to the drunk's glee. He shut out the man's barrage of taunts as he hunted for a weak spot in the cell. Some straps had rusted. He might worry them loose and get out onto the top. From there he could wiggle between iron rods and jail ceiling to the front and drop down. He didn't know if the marshal kept the door leading to his office locked. If he did, it would take a bit of waiting for the marshal to open it, but sooner or later he would.

A meal, some other reason, but he would come through. When he did, Slocum knew he would have only one chance. He stared hard at the grizzled old man in the other cage and knew he had to get rid of him. The drunk would warn the marshal of any breakout attempt.

Slocum jumped when the marshal came into the tight area in front of the cells. He opened the other door and chased the drunk out. Then he turned and said to Slocum, "You got a visitor."

"Who?"

Past the lawman Slocum saw Polly Greene standing in the outer office, nervously fidgeting with her purse.

"Get on in. Be careful, miss. He's a desperate man." The marshal didn't close the door. Instead, he pulled his chair around and sat so he could watch everything happening inside the cellblock.

"John!" Polly rushed to the door and looped her fingers around the thick metal straps. "I'm so sorry!"

"I didn't do it," Slocum said, futile anger building in him. "I saw Haskell at the mine, but I didn't kill him. He was busy salting the mine. The guy who found him might have—"

"No, I don't think so, John. The man is well respected. I can't remember his name, but he has a reputation for being honest—and he doesn't even carry a gun. Whoever killed Haskell shot him once in the back of the head."

"Ash Wallings tried to dry-gulch me. Maybe the marshal ought to ask him a few questions."

"They think it was Haskell who shot at you." Polly reached out and touched the side of his head where Wallings's bullet had creased him. "They know about the argument on the train. Several other passengers who got off at Corinne told the marshal. And they know you lied to others about your business here."

"The businessmen from San Francisco," Slocum said, a sinking feeling in his gut. "And their mining expert."

"They told the marshal about it and the gentleman from Salt Lake City, the one who found Haskell's body, said you and Haskell were not on the best of terms. They seem to have convicted you on the basis of nothing but hearsay evidence!" The way Polly stared at him made Slocum mad. It was as if she said the words but didn't quite believe them—or him.

"I didn't kill him," Slocum said flatly. "I've got to get out of here."

"Professor Malloy will take care of it, John," she said. Seeing his disgusted expression, Polly added, "The professor is a very good lawyer. He has degrees in many fields. Paleontology is only his most recent passion. He knows physics and chemistry and even classical languages. That is what interested him in legal studies.''

Slocum snorted at the notion of the dapper Hercules Malloy defending him in a rough-and-tumble western court of law. But he had to be better than anyone in Corinne willing to tackle his case. A frontier lawyer would only help put the noose around his neck.

''Tell the professor to get this done as quickly as he can,'' Slocum said, seeing the marshal stand and come to the door. He knew the time allotted Polly was up. ''And thank you for believing me.''

''I do, John. You could never kill anyone. Not by shooting him in the back!'' Polly recoiled a little when the marshal took her arm to usher her from the cells. Then she hurried off to tell Professor Malloy everything Slocum had said.

Slocum waited for the marshal to retreat to his office before he got to work on the rusty iron straps. It wasn't that he had no confidence in Professor Malloy. Slocum just believed in having an alternative to a necktie party.

''Your honor,'' Professor Malloy said pompously as he rose from the table, ''I want to move for a complete dismissal of charges against Mr. Slocum.''

''Who are you and why are you tellin' me what to do?'' growled the judge. His florid face turned a little redder, and the way he hunkered down reminded Slocum of a bulldog ready to rip the throat out of anyone venturing too close.

''I am Professor Hercules Malloy, J.D., of Harvard University in Cambridge.''

''Easterner,'' said the judge. ''You got a law degree?''

Slocum restrained Malloy before the small man responded to the verbal challenge. Slocum wasn't sure, but he thought the professor had already said he had a degree. Those fancy initials had to mean something.

''I do, Your Honor.''

"Then let's get on with it." The judge turned to the prosecutor, a youngish man with a stack of law books beside him on the table. "Tell us why you want this critter's neck stretched, Davey."

"Sure, Pa, I mean, Your Honor."

Slocum closed his eyes and groaned. He didn't have a ghost of a chance now. The Corinne prosecutor was the judge's son. Slocum wondered if the marshal was also related.

"We found a Mr. Joe Haskell dead at the Lovely Lady Mine. Slocum was inquirin' after Mr. Haskell a few hours before the body was found. Haskell was shot smack in the head. Right about here." He almost got his arm out of joint reaching around to point to the back of his skull.

"And?" urged the judge.

"That's about it. We got witnesses that says there was bad blood between 'em."

"Sounds like enough to me," the judge said. He lifted his gavel to rap it smartly but hesitated when Malloy rose. For being a banty rooster in size, Hercules Malloy projected quite an air of authority.

"My turn, Your Honor. We can dispense with a lot of this evidence as being worthless."

"You tellin' me what my boy said is a lie?"

"No, Your Honor, not a lie. Just incomplete. Mr. Slocum's business dealings with Haskell were consummated on the train to Corinne. Haskell owed him money and paid promptly upon demand. We have witnesses to that." Malloy glanced over at the prosecutor.

"Some said they saw Haskell giving him money," admitted the prosecutor.

"Mr. Slocum's interest in Haskell revolved less around the man than on what he was selling. Mr. Haskell was acting as agent for Tork Beckworuth and Gold Tooth Lawton in selling the mine." Again came a nod from the prosecutor. "What caliber was the bullet that killed Joe Haskell?"

"Caliber? I don't know. I got the hunk of lead here somewhere." The prosecutor fumbled in his pocket and dropped it on the table for Malloy. The small man held it high and squinted as he looked at it.

"This is not a bullet from a six-shooter, at least not Mr. Slocum's. If you will examine it carefully, you will see it is from a shotgun, double-ought in load. This would indicate Mr. Haskell died from an errant shotgun blast, not by action of my client's six-gun."

"Give that to me." The judge rolled the piece of lead around. "You're right. But we don't know if Slocum used a shotgun on the varmint."

"We don't know if *you* did, either, Your Honor." Malloy held up his hand to forestall the sharp rap of the gavel. "I mean no disrespect. All I am saying is, anyone could have done it. No one saw Mr. Slocum shoot Haskell, a man with whom he had already transacted a successful business deal."

"You sayin' Slocum and Haskell might have done business again in the future?" asked the prosecutor.

"Why not?"

The judge's face turned into deep furrows and dark glares. "Your jibe about me maybe doing the crime hits home, Shorty. Just because Slocum knew Haskell before they came to Corinne doesn't mean squat. Haskell didn't make many friends in town."

"Several people saw Ash Wallings and Elias Kenyon arguing with him. That is not to say they committed the crime. Rather, it shows Mr. Haskell had a history of contentiousness and might have, uh, rubbed anyone in Corinne the wrong way."

"Davey, you got real evidence in this case or are you just blowin' smoke out your butt?"

"Pa, Your Honor, this is all the marshal gave me!"

"I can't hold a man for trial when nobody much liked the deceased and there's no proof the defendant used a scattergun on him. Case dismissed for lack of evidence.'' The judge pounded his gavel and stalked out of the tiny room.

Slocum leaned back and wiped sweat from his forehead. "How did you know Haskell had argued with Wallings?" he asked.

"I made inquiries around town. Interestingly, they fought over Wallings's declaration of a monster living in Bear Lake," the professor said. In a lower voice, he added, "Also, you mentioned it to Miss Greene. I had no need to inquire beyond such an unimpeachable source."

"Thanks, professor," Slocum said. "I owe you for this."

"Tut, tut, there's nothing to this. If it had gone to trial, convincing a jury might have been more difficult. These preliminary hearings are normally nothing but folderol. And I certainly could not let a valuable employee such as yourself rot in territorial jail. We have a creature to find!"

Professor Malloy tentatively slapped Slocum on the back, smiled almost shyly, and bustled off. Slocum didn't know what to make of the scholar. At times he seemed afraid of his own shadow, then he doggedly launched an attack against the powers that be in Corinne's legal circles. And when Slocum thought Malloy was totally engrossed in his own concerns, he showed he had been observing closely everything around him.

Slocum figured he owed Malloy one monster out in Bear Lake and it was time to find it.

13

"It's too late to do much hunting today," Slocum said. For the past half hour he had guided the buckboard across deep ruts increasingly hidden by long shadows cast by the setting sun. "If we go on much longer in the twilight, we're going to break an axle. The load is too heavy for this small a buckboard, and I'm having trouble even keeping to what passes for a road."

"We need the equipment," was all the professor said. Beside Slocum, he peered down at his notes, as if the drawing there might pop off the page and come alive.

"Setting it up in the morning will be a sight easier than blundering around in the dark. Getting camp established is going to be chore enough for tonight." Slocum shivered as a strong wind whipped across the surface of Bear Lake and carried a hint of forgotten winter with it. He welcomed the change from Corinne's heat, and he welcomed the freedom he still had. Rotting in the town's hoosegow wasn't the way he intended to spend the rest of his life.

"Very well, Mr. Slocum. Let me make this perfectly clear, however. I can hardly restrain myself." Professor Malloy jumped from the buckboard and walked about the small clearing on top of the ridge, peering down at the lake as if

by force of will he could make his creature appear. It didn't.
He shoved his walking stick into a soft spot of dirt and hunkered down, pinning a map to the ground in front of him
with four rocks. He took out a set of dividers and carefully
walked off the distances across and around the lake as if he
were a sea captain about to go around the Cape.

Slocum helped Polly from the buckboard, then tended to
his dappled gray gelding that had trotted along behind, content to be riderless for the entire trip from town. Slocum had
half a mind to ride on out, but he couldn't do it. He owed
Malloy for arguing his case in front of the judge and getting
him off so quickly. The charges had been trumped up, and
the marshal had been happy to find someone to blame. Now
that he had a murder on his hands, the lawman needed another culprit. Slocum worried that the marshal might find
new evidence that would somehow link him to Haskell's
killing.

Slocum had seen too many lawmen grab onto a victim and
then find only evidence pointing in one direction. It made
life easier and kept the townspeople believing their law was
the best anywhere. Like as not, the victim of such a hunt
was considered undesirable by most of the citizens.

Slocum hadn't been around Corinne enough to generate
such an opinion of himself, but small towns were notoriously
suspicious of strangers, even a town like Corinne that was
filled with railroad workers and other transients. If anything,
that footloose quality of most of the people coming through
the city made the residents even more spooked when
someone died, especially by a gunshot to the back of the
head.

"I'll help unload the equipment," Polly offered. "I know
where it ought to go."

"I can tend to it," Slocum said. "Most of it is pretty
heavy."

"I know," the lovely blond said, smiling. "I packed it.

The professor had other things on his mind before we left Boston.''

''He thinks he can pinpoint where the creature is, using that map?'' Slocum grunted as he heaved a large crate from the back of the buckboard. Staggering a few steps, he put it down with a heavy thud. He didn't know what was inside, but it had to be mostly iron to weigh so much.

''We know where its lair is. From that point it must— John, what's that?'' Polly grabbed his arm and spun toward the lake. Her face turned pale at the mournful sound, then her face lit up with excitement. ''John, it's the creature again!''

Slocum had heard foghorns around San Francisco Bay make similar sounds. The note hung in the air, then dipped before rising again to a pitch that caused Slocum's ears to ring. Visions of creatures fighting and dying came to mind as he listened. A slight whistling signaled the end of the cry.

''You heard it, too!'' cried Malloy. The professor rushed over to join Slocum and his assistant. ''That can only be my creature, mine, mine!''

''Get the telescope set up,'' urged Polly. ''In this box. We must make a sighting. That will tell us what we need to know about its species!'' She tugged futilely at the rough planking on the side of the box. Slocum lent a hand and broke off the board. Polly pulled out a long tube and the professor fumbled about until he had a tripod set up.

''We can see most of the lake from this vantage,'' Malloy said, squinting into the eyepiece. He began scanning back and forth along the murky shoreline and across the choppy water of Bear Lake. Beside him, Polly stood vigilantly, trying to locate any movement before her mentor.

The mournful lowing sounded, more like a cow than any monster Slocum could imagine. He went to his saddle and dragged out the Winchester from the sheath. Both Polly and the professor were too engrossed in their hunt to notice him leaving camp.

Slocum made his way down the slope of the crater holding Bear Lake, the path more difficult by the minute. When he went through a thick stand of trees, fragrant pine needles crushed under his feet, muffling his advance. Slocum didn't think he needed to be too silent, but he felt better knowing only a sharp-eared creature would hear his approach.

Reaching the shore, he cocked the rifle. The professor wanted the beast alive. Slocum had other ideas. Anything big enough to make those noises wasn't something he wanted to meet without a gun in his hands.

Slocum turned from side to side, listening hard for sounds of a sea monster. The foghorn sounds rolled over the water, causing Slocum to shift away from the direction he faced. He frowned. Unless he was terribly mistaken, the monster's song came from the direction of Beckwourth and Lawton's mine or the back side of the hill where they had burrowed for gold.

Picking his way carefully along the water's edge, Slocum kept an eye peeled for any movement. He saw quite a few rabbits coming to the lake to drink and at least one predator sniffing after them. Slocum turned his attention away from such small game and set his sights for bigger targets—much bigger.

He crossed the rocky peninsula sticking into Bear Lake and started along a path familiar to him now. Over this hill lay Gold Tooth Lawton and Tork Beckwourth's mine. He felt a little uneasy, remembering how Beckwourth had ambushed him so easily on the game trail. He paused and strained for any sound of another hunter moving in the night. For a moment, nothing but the wind and waves came to him. Then the usual nighttime noises came back as the animals went about their business.

"Nothing human moving out there," he said softly to himself. Slocum pushed on toward the distant spot where the monster must have been when it caterwauled. The shoreline grew ragged and jutted in and out, forming small coves able to hide anything the size of a frigate.

Less than ten minutes of stalking brought him to the mouth of an inlet. Without conscious thought, Slocum lifted his rifle, put it to his shoulder, and fired in a smooth action. In the distance came a bellowing, almost human, followed by the mournful foghorn voice of the creature they had seen so dimly. Slocum fired again at the dark outline ahead of him.

Then he cursed.

As if the monster had slipped under the water, it simply vanished from sight. He thought he had hit his target, whatever it might have been. There hadn't been a satisfying thud of lead striking flesh, but Slocum knew he had hit something. He *felt* it. All his days spent as a sniper during the war had given him the innate sense of right and wrong, hit or miss, when it came to marksmanship.

"I hit it," Slocum said to himself. His own voice reassured him that the world hadn't changed. "But what is *it*?"

Slocum advanced along the shore, entering the cove cautiously. If he had wounded a large reptile, he didn't want to be on the receiving end of a vicious attack as it struggled to protect itself. But after Slocum had completely circled the cove and found nothing, he had to stop and scratch his head in wonder. He had hit it. He knew he had. But the moonless night and the wind and the heavy clouds masking the stars plunged the cove into a pitch-darkness preventing him from finding any spoor.

Slocum retraced his steps, even more wary than before. Again he found nothing. Disgruntled at the failure, he trudged back to the distant rise where Professor Malloy and Polly Greene had set up their telescope. Maybe they had seen where the creature went after he shot it.

"Slocum! There you are," cried Professor Malloy. "Was that you shooting?"

"I saw it and got off a couple rounds," Slocum admitted. "I'm not sure if I hit it, though. I thought I did, but—"

"*I want it alive!*" Malloy screeched. "How dare you jeopardize my expedition like this?"

"Sorry," Slocum apologized, not sorry at all. "The inlet where I sighted it isn't too far away. In the morning we can go down and track the monster from there." He had lingering doubts about what he had shot at. He had seen only a moving silhouette—but such a huge, towering figure it had been! What else could it have been but a sea monster come to live in Bear Lake?

Slocum looked around and asked, "Where's Polly?"

"I don't know. The silly girl might have gone off to find you, to tell you how aggrieved I am that you shot at my creature."

"She's gone?" Slocum felt a cold lump knot in his stomach. "Down to the lake?"

"I don't know. I was scanning the lake for any trace of the creature. I heard her mutter something, then she rushed off."

"After I'd fired?"

"Yes, yes," the professor cried. "Now, let me get to my observations. This is important work. The weather conditions, how the beast might swim, does it go underwater, all that must be recorded for further study."

Slocum said nothing as he headed back downhill. If Polly had gone to find him, she would get turned around and be lost within minutes. The utter darkness of the night made tracking almost impossible and convinced Slocum the city-bred woman had no chance of finding him by herself. No trace of her showed on the track down the side of the hill, but when Slocum got to the water, he saw she had gone in the direction opposite to the one he had taken.

That didn't surprise him unduly. Sound turned tricky along the water. With so many rocky crags around the lake to reflect sound, he knew how easily she could have mistaken his location. He hurried along the water, going farther away from the professor's camp and growing increasingly edgy when he didn't find Polly right away.

But he continued finding traces of recent passage. A footprint in the mud, slowly filling with water, a piece of cloth torn by a blackberry bush, even the curious silence of the animals along the lake all told Slocum someone had come this way not long before.

He held his tongue, though, and did not call out to her. He had the eerie feeling of being watched. Several times Slocum stopped and listened hard, trying to locate Polly by the crash of her passage. No sound reached his sharp ears. What worried him more were the tiny noises he did hear— and they were not natural.

Slocum tried to put a name to the soft creaking and failed. Something in the lake or across it continually warned him of danger, but he didn't see anything. For that Slocum was relieved. He had shot some beast, something big, and didn't want it coming after him or Polly. It could only be wounded and mad as hell.

Away from the lake, uphill from his position, Slocum heard twigs cracking and a muffled voice. He made sure his rifle had a shell in the chamber, then cut across a grassy area and entered the woods above the lake. It had been dark before. Now Slocum thought he had been dipped into an inkwell. Relying more on sound and feel than sight, he made his way through the dense undergrowth, stopping occasionally to listen and be sure he wasn't getting turned around. If he kept the upward slope on his right, he knew he wasn't likely to walk in a giant circle.

As if by magic, he suddenly entered a spacious glen stretching uphill and across the side of the mountain. Wildflowers filled the air with fragrance, and he heard a murmuring he recognized instantly.

"Polly!" he called. "Where are you? It's me, Slocum!" His words echoed across the open space. He saw movement a hundred yards away.

"John, over here! I wondered if I would ever find you!"

Slocum made his way through the flowers and finally stood beside her. He had heard the woman reciting poetry about the wildflowers. No one else on this mountainside was likely to be doing that. She had plucked a dozen blossoms and sniffed them in deep appreciation.

But Polly quickly dropped them when Slocum got close enough. She threw her arms around him and hugged him tight.

"I was so worried. The gunshots. You were gone. Oh, I was so afraid for you!" She clung to him until Slocum wasn't sure if she would ever let go. When she did, Slocum took her hand and pulled her to the ground. They sat in the middle of the field, surrounded by summertime blooms.

"It's a good thing I returned to camp," he told her. "You went in the opposite direction from where I took a shot at the monster."

"You saw it? You didn't hurt it, did you? The professor will be so angry!" Her tone told Slocum she wouldn't be too pleased, either. Her moment of glory, albeit reflected from Professor Malloy, would vanish with a clean kill.

"I couldn't find any evidence that I hit it," Slocum said. Polly relaxed. "It was foolish to rush off like that. You don't know your way around these woods. There might not be grizzlies here like the marshal claims, but there are other dangerous animals."

She shivered at the thought of wolves and snuggled closer. Slocum laid his rifle beside him and put both arms around her shoulders. She quaked with fear.

"It'll be all right," he said. "It's going to be a chore

returning to camp tonight. The darkness is damned near complete.''

''I know. I thought to get a little higher and see if I couldn't spot you from the heights. That's when I entered the forest. I made a mistake, didn't I?''

''It's all right,'' he said, looking down into her pale face. In spite of the intense darkness, her hair glowed like fine gold. He bent over and kissed her. Polly responded immediately.

She swarmed up and pulled him back onto the ground. She half lay on top of him kissing and tonguing, her fingers moving here and there to produce incredible sensations in his loins.

''We shouldn't,'' he said. ''It is dangerous out here.''

''I'll cry out when we're making love, John,'' she said in a husky voice. ''That'll frighten the animals away.''

''Or draw them to see what the commotion is all about,'' he said, grinning crookedly. He kissed her again, abandoning any attempt to convince her this wasn't the right time or place. Somehow, the world had changed and it was all right now. He shucked off his gun belt and Polly unbuttoned his fly.

He moaned softly as his throbbing manhood sprang out of its cloth prison. The cool night wind across aroused flesh sent shivers up his spine. The cold vanished instantly and was replaced by Polly's eager mouth. She engulfed him and began using her tongue to drive him crazy with need.

He arched his back slightly, trying to shove more of himself into her mouth. Her fingers stroked on the sides of his shaft and tickled his balls. Inside, he churned and boiled. Slocum reached down and laced his fingers in her gorgeous blond hair, guiding her in the up-and-down motion he desired most.

This was good enough for a few minutes, but he had to have more. Gently, he pulled her away from his crotch and turned her around. She instinctively knew what he wanted—perhaps because she desired the same thing. Polly threw her leg over his body and settled down.

He gasped when he felt himself slipping into her heated interior.

"You're not wearing anything under that skirt," he accused.

"Are you glad?" she taunted. Polly wiggled her hips from side to side and sent new tremors into his body. Slocum decided it was time to give her as much pleasure as she was giving him. Reaching up, he shoved the mounds of her breasts into the palms of his hands. Squeezing lightly, he began to rotate them.

Polly closed her eyes and lifted and fell on the thick pole within her lust-moistened interior. Like a colt, she tossed her head back. The gentle wind caught her hair and carried it away like a golden banner. Lurching and turning, she worked up and down on Slocum until the friction burned away his control.

He squeezed down harder on her breasts, feeling the taut nipples beneath his fingers throbbing with passion. His hands slipped away and circled her waist, shoving her down hard with every downstroke she made. She began moaning softly, and Slocum knew from the tightness around him she was on the brink.

His hands roamed up and down her body, tweaking her nipples, stroking her cheek, slipping across her lips. Polly rose and fell, driving the thick spike of Slocum's manhood ever deeper into her. As he stroked her face, she gasped, stiffened, and then went berserk. Almost faster than Slocum could tolerate, she lifted and fell on him, her hips grinding powerfully. A shudder passed through her body and into his.

He erupted like a volcano. Together, they surged and soared and blended body and soul before collapsing weak and sated to lie in each other's arms.

"I never felt this before, John," she whispered into his ear. Somehow, Polly managed to snuggle even closer.

Before Slocum could reply, a distant moaning like a foghorn filled the air. The Bear Lake monster again swam in its private preserve.

14

Slocum sat up and looked around. The field in which he and Polly had spent the night was more exposed than he had thought. During the dense night he hadn't seen how vulnerable they were. He disengaged his arm from under Polly's head and picked up the rifle. The sun poked up over the treetops and told Slocum they ought to be on the move. Professor Malloy must be beside himself with worry.

Then Slocum wondered if Malloy had even noticed their absence. The dapper scholar had been so engrossed in his hunt for the monster, he might not notice anything smaller than a large house.

"John?" Polly sat up, looking around in fright. "There you are. I thought you had gone, and it frightened me."

"We'd better get on down to the lake and find our way back to camp. I've got enough kinks in my back from sleeping on the cold ground to last me a lifetime."

Polly reached high above her head and arched her back. Slocum thought of a sinuous cat stretching in the warm sun. He admired the flow of the blond's body, the way the muscles played just right, and the sight of all the enticingly soft curves.

"You are right. I hope the professor has spotted the creature. If not, we should explore the lair more carefully. There is so much to do. I can hardly wait to get started doing it!''

He helped her to her feet. She brushed off her skirt and shook her head at the dirty spots. Together they left the meadow and meandered downhill to the lake. Slocum's belly growled in hunger. He was long past a meal, but forgoing a feast or two meant little when he thought of the time he had spent with Polly.

"Up there is the camp," he said, but his eyes traveled along the shore toward the rocky peninsula where the monster's lair was—and beyond to where he thought he had hit the creature.

"What's wrong, John?" She tried to see what he did and failed. "Did you see something?"

"Last night, when I fired," he said. "I think I hit it but couldn't find any sign in the dark."

"I'm hungry," Polly admitted, "but I want to know what happened. Let's go look so we can better report to Professor Malloy."

"All right, but if we come across it, you stay behind me. I don't want you getting in the line of fire." Slocum hefted his rifle, wondering if it was a powerful enough weapon to stop a monster as big as the one he thought he had fired at. He doubted it.

Side by side, Slocum and Polly Greene hiked along Bear Lake until they reached the cove where Slocum had trapped the monster.

"In there. It rose up and I fired," he told her. "Stay here while I—"

"I will do no such thing!" Polly exclaimed.

Slocum knew better than to argue. He set off at a brisk pace, avoiding the edge of the water while keeping a sharp lookout for any spoor. He stood stock-still as he stared at the debris washing onto the shore at his feet. Slocum knelt and picked up a splintered piece of wood. Two nails had torn loose from something bigger. A piece of the larger structure still remained and to it had been tacked a torn piece of dark cloth.

"What is it?"

"I'm not sure," Slocum said, handing it to Polly. He walked along the shore and picked up two more pieces of splintery wood. One had a bullet hole shot through it—a hole about the size made by a slug from his rifle.

He had hit something the night before, and it wasn't flesh and blood. Slocum said nothing to Polly of his suspicions, but it appeared that someone was hoodwinking the professor. Or was it only Malloy on the receiving end of this hoax? The Mormon family had said the monster appeared about six months earlier, just at spring thaw.

"When did Malloy decide to come out and find the Bear Lake monster?" Slocum asked.

"Why, several months ago he read in the *Deseret News* of a new sighting. We began digging through older articles and found Mr. Rich's earlier writings. Discreet inquiries convinced Professor Malloy that there was something important here."

"But no direct evidence before this spring?"

"Why, I don't know. The professor kept much of the background data from me. It would not do to let others have access to it."

"No, I reckon not," Slocum said, his mind turning down other paths. "Is there any money involved? Would the professor pay a big reward to anyone finding the monster?"

"Why, no, I think not. This is a scientific expedition. We do not purchase information. We collect it ourselves. We're willing to pay people such as yourself for their services. Or Dark Cloud." Polly turned solemn at the thought of the Paiute scout.

Slocum didn't think the professor would pony up a reward to anyone promising to deliver the monster. Such an offer would offend the scholar's sense of honor. Besides, Slocum thought the scheme far too complicated. Who would fake a monster, leak the information to a professor at Harvard, and then not immediately contact Malloy when he arrived in Corinne? For a confidence game, it was too chancy with no real promise of gaining money from Professor Malloy.

"Do you think we saw only a frame covered with dark cloth?" Polly had finally put together the facts and had come to the same conclusion Slocum had.

"No reason I can see," he said truthfully. Slocum left the lakeshore and started up the hill. Trying to get his bearings proved easier now that he had spent some time exploring the area. Over this hill Tork Beckwourth and Gold Tooth Lawton had their mine, but the worn path Slocum spotted didn't run up and over the hill. It meandered off around the hill with no evidence that it ever ran to the crest of the ridge.

"But if it is a fake, we are hunting for something that does not exist." Polly sounded outraged. Slocum was more curious than angry—if this was a deception—and he thought it was.

"You up to a little more hiking?" Slocum pointed out the trail.

"Of course, if it will answer the question concerning the creature's existence," Polly said almost primly. Slocum knew the bubble would be burst if he found evidence of a phony beast in the lake. How Polly and her mentor would react was a question Slocum pushed aside. He was more interested in the truth than writing scholarly papers on some brute that should have died out hundreds of years earlier.

The dirt path was well used. Here and there he saw distinct imprints of a bootheel. Dropping to one knee, Slocum saw where at least two different men had walked this path recently. He also found more fresh splinters, as if the damaged frame down in the lake had been moved uphill.

"More cloth, John," spoke up Polly. She had gone a few

feet farther along the path and had found a piece of dark sailcloth.

''Stay behind me. This might be more dangerous than I thought.'' Slocum clutched the Winchester in his hand as he pushed along the path. It led not to the top of the hillside but along the back, giving occasional views of Bear Lake through the dense trees.

He held out his hand and stopped Polly when he saw small piles of crushed rock. He kicked at the pile and saw the kind of debris that usually accumulated in mine tailings. Slocum walked a few yards more along the path and saw the crevice in the side of the hill.

''What is it, John? It looks like a crevice.''

''It is,'' he said. The cut in the hillside was natural, but the look of the ground just inside the opening was not. Thousands of steps had pressed the dirt into a hard floor. Two small metal buckets, dented from long use, showed how the tailings had been removed from the mine—and Slocum had no doubt that a mine was what he had discovered.

''Polly, get up there in the underbrush and hide. I'm going to do some exploring and don't want you in the way.''

''I've come this far, John. Even if this might prove dangerous, I—''

''No,'' he said sharply. ''If someone is sailing a fake monster onto the lake, they are trying to scare folks away. That means they'll likely not draw the line at killing.''

Beckwourth and Lawton!

''Might be,'' Slocum said, but he didn't think so. He remembered another attack. ''Stay here while I search inside the mine. I won't take long.'' He saw her hidden in the thick bushes growing just above the crevice. Walking back and forth, he tried to catch any sight of the hidden woman. When he was satisfied she was out of sight, he slipped between the sharp stones protecting the mouth of the cave.

His instincts had been right. Picks and shovels lined the

wall, lots of them as if the work had stretched out for a long time. Slocum found a half dozen carbide lamps. He ignited the first one he picked up with enough water in it. For a moment, he considered taking a second lamp, remembering what had happened in the Lovely Lady Mine. Slocum shook his head. He was getting spooked for no good reason.

Slowly making his way deeper into the mine, he passed the narrow corridor and found a wider area, one painstakingly chipped from the solid rock. On the ground stretched narrow ore cart tracks. Slocum held up the light and tried to see the end of the track. He couldn't.

Curiosity running out of control, Slocum went deeper into the mine. Now and then he checked the walls for any sign of ore. The milky quartz around a thick vein told him of significant gold in this claim. It had been chipped out long since, but the tunnel followed the vein straight into the hillside.

Slocum walked faster until he reached a section where the roof forced him to bend double. Dropping to a crouch, he examined stacks of Salt Lake City newspapers piled along the tracks. The oldest dated back more than eighteen months. From the debris left around the newspapers, Slocum could tell that someone had eaten well while reading. Whiskey bottles long since drained lined the far wall. Empty burlap bags hinted at large quantities of food brought in to keep the miners from needing to leave until the end of their shift.

''Shift.'' Slocum snorted. ''This is no company operation. But what the hell *is* it?''

At the end of the track, he found recent evidence of work on the veins of ore holding the precious metal. Slocum used the tip of a pick to scrape out a hunk of rock. It popped into his hand and he examined it carefully. He needed an assay done, but this ore might prove out to four or five ounces a ton, a fabulous amount for any mine.

''Not Beckwourth and Lawton's mine, that's for sure,''

he said, looking around the tiny chamber at the back of the mine. "But whose mine is it? Wallings? Kenyon?"

Even if this were so, it didn't explain why Ash Wallings had taken to back-shooting and wanted Slocum dead. Slocum had known nothing of this mine until a few minutes ago. Too many questions lacked answers. First, he needed to know what the hell was going on around Bear Lake.

He twisted around and stared at the ceiling of the mine, his eyes widening. He had thought the wealth of the mine lay in the vein he had followed along the tunnel, but the rocky ceiling held real pay dirt. He scraped his thumbnail over it repeatedly until he worried off a hunk, shining with a small amount of pure gold.

"Maybe this is where Tork Beckwourth got his nugget," Slocum mumbled. It hardly made any sense that Beckwourth and Lawton would mine on both sides of the hill, boasting about gold from this mine while the Lovely Lady was only marginally profitable. Or perhaps it did. Maybe the two miners intended to sell their worthless mine and keep working this wildly profitable one.

"Too many questions; no answers," Slocum said aloud. And none of it explained the stranger goings-on with the monster in the lake.

As Slocum started back, he heard rocks tumbling. He leveled his rifle, peering toward the mouth of the mine. More sounds came from outside, followed by a piercing scream.

"Polly!"

Slocum rushed from the mine, swinging his rifle around. He found no target. He stumbled, got his feet under him, and worked up the hillside to where he had left Polly.

Gone! Polly Greene was gone!

15

Slocum started to call out Polly's name, then stopped. Whatever had happened outside the mine had been like lightning, coming quickly and leaving behind only a small clap of thunder: her single cry for help. Slocum knew better than to draw attention to himself by shouting for her to reply. If she could, she would be screaming at the top of her lungs right now.

Slocum studied the ground where the woman had crouched in hiding. He had no trouble seeing the distinct imprint of her shoes in the soft dirt. But the ground farther uphill turned rocky and left no print. He thought he found dollops of mud from her shoes scraped off on the rock, but he could not be sure.

Of a track he found nothing. Slocum ranged farther, moving in a fan-shaped track, trying to find any trace of her. He gave up after almost an hour of hunting. On impulse, he hiked to the top of the hill and made his way around until he came to a halt just above Tork Beckwourth and Gold Tooth Lawton's mine. The Lovely Lady Mine stood as empty as it had before. Slocum wasn't sure what he expected to find there. Possibly Polly and her captor.

The silence from below mocked him.

He waited a few minutes to be sure the blond student's kidnappers weren't lying in wait. He didn't hear a single sound to indicate they were below him. Edging around on the hillside, he got a look into the mouth of the mine. Some middling digging had opened another few feet, but if Polly had been hidden away, it wasn't inside the Lovely Lady Mine.

Disgusted with himself, Slocum went back to the top of the ridge and made his way through the pines and junipers until he reached Professor Malloy's camp. The small man bustled about, looking flustered.

"Mr. Slocum," Malloy called upon seeing him. "Where have you been?"

"You see Polly?" Slocum demanded. He had no time for small talk.

"Miss Greene? I thought she might be with you. I tried to remember what you—she—said last night. I was so excited, everything blurred together. Did she not go in search of you after hearing gunshots? Yes, yes, she did!"

"You haven't seen her today?"

"No," the professor said, eyes widening. "What has happened, sir? Tell me!"

Slocum did the best he could to relate his and Polly's strange journey to the mine and what happened there. He left out the part about finding the splintered wood and sailcloth. That would only distract the professor from finding Polly Greene.

"Should we return to this spot and search further?" The professor scratched his chin, then fetched his walking stick as if he intended to set off right away.

Slocum glanced at the sun. It was well past midday already. The pair of them would have little luck finding her. Worse, her kidnappers could have spirited her a dozen miles away by now, although Slocum didn't think so. The secrets to be unearthed were at Bear Lake, not anywhere far off.

"We need help. Finding her by ourselves isn't likely." Slocum didn't want to insult the professor by telling him that if a trained frontiersman couldn't find any spoor, a Harvard professor was even less likely to do so.

"The creature," muttered Malloy. "Might the creature have seized her?" His eyes widened in horror.

"Don't think it's too likely," Slocum said. "Seems as if the monster only comes out at night—"

"Nocturnal, yes, it seems to be a denizen of the night," cut in Professor Malloy.

"So it wouldn't be out in broad daylight. Whatever's happened doesn't involve the monster, at least not directly." Slocum's mind turned over the facts and kept coming up with too many unanswered questions.

"Ride back to Corinne, Mr. Slocum. Fetch the marshal. Get a posse! I shall pay them well. Here, here is fifty dollars. Hire as many men as possible. If Miss Greene has fallen into some hideous crevice and is lying unconscious, we must find her as quickly as possible."

Slocum took the money and stuffed it into his shirt pocket. "I can get into town pretty fast if I ride hard," he told the professor. "Use that spyglass of yours to keep a sharp lookout, especially over near the monster's lair. I'll be back before sundown."

"Yes, yes, very well. Do hurry, Mr. Slocum. I don't know what I would do without Miss Greene's able assistance. She is quite special, unique among my students."

Slocum wasted no time listening to the scholar's maundering. He jumped onto his gray and rode off at a pace intended to get him into Corinne as quickly as possible without killing the horse under him.

Slocum made it into town two hours before sunset and rode straight to the marshal's office. He jumped from the gray and went back into the calaboose, a small shudder passing through him. If the lawman hadn't found anyone to blame for Joe Haskell's murder, he might still have his sights set on John Slocum.

The marshal looked up from a stack of papers spread on

his desk. "What do you want, Slocum?"

Slocum explained quickly what had happened. The marshal snorted and spat, hemmed, hawed, and tried to figure a way out of getting a posse to hunt for the lost woman. Only when Slocum mentioned the professor's offer of fifty dollars did the marshal respond.

"Reckon something ought to be done," the lawman said, pushing away from the desk and grabbing a rifle from a rack near his desk. "I'll round up a few gents, and we'll scour those hills. The terrain is rugged, but we can get it done, with enough help."

"Not before sundown," Slocum said. "We can't get back before dark. Would there be any point in hunting then?"

"I'll get a posse lined up, and we'll be off first thing in the morning."

Slocum clenched his fists. It was reasonable to wait until morning, but he felt that Polly's life hung in the balance.

"Get them together, ride out to the professor's camp, and then they can start the search at first light. There's no trouble getting out to Bear Lake. It'll only be in the woods after dark there's any problem."

"For fifty dollars, I might have a string of men a mile long out there," the marshal said. "Get yourself a drink and I'll round them up. I'll let you know when we're ready to ride, Slocum."

Slocum thought the lawman sounded almost sympathetic. He nodded brusquely and went to Ben's Drink Emporium for some tarantula juice. The liquor tasted like piss in his mouth, and Slocum knew he couldn't take another. He left and swung into the saddle, waiting for the marshal to get the promised posse. He saw a half dozen men around the lawman, but someone out toward the far side of Corinne caught his eye.

"Kenyon," he muttered. Slocum urged his tired horse down an alley, through the back ways of Corinne, and then again to the main street where he had seen the man. He caught faint wisps of argument and turned. He couldn't see who Elias Kenyon quarreled with, being entirely hidden by shadows, but the debate threatened to turn violent. Kenyon balled his fists and stepped forward.

As quickly as Kenyon's temper flared, it died. Slocum heard him say, "All right, you danged fool. I'll do it, but this is on your head if it don't work out!"

Kenyon stormed past Slocum, going straight for the marshal. Slocum turned his horse in the direction of the man Kenyon had fought with, thinking it might be Ash Wallings. If it was, Slocum wanted to finish the fight that the man had started. But Slocum found no trace of anyone and could not pursue the tracking because the marshal summoned him.

"Get your butt on over here, Slocum. We're goin' on out to the professor's camp now. You got to show us the way so we don't get lost."

This produced some wry comments from the six men in the posse about the marshal's tracking skills. Slocum's eyes went straight to Elias Kenyon, mounted and ready to ride with the posse.

"What's he doing here? He and Wallings tried to bushwhack me," Slocum said coldly.

"Kenyon knows the area. He volunteered. Don't go causin' any trouble, Slocum. All we got is your word that he and Wallings tried to gun you down."

"You got it all wrong, Slocum," piped up Kenyon. "All I want to do is find the little lady before the monster gets her. It's downright dangerous out by Bear Lake!" He glanced from side to side to see how the others in the posse reacted. Slocum couldn't help noticing one of them moved his horse away and slipped off into the twilight, not wanting anything to do with a lake-living monster.

Curiosity began to get the better of Slocum. "All right. If you vouch for him, marshal, that's good enough for me." But Slocum made sure he didn't ride with Elias Kenyon at his back.

They reached the professor's bivouac before midnight, pitched camp, and then began the search for Polly Greene at sunup.

"She vanished on me up there," Slocum said, pointing up the path toward the mine he had discovered.

"Might have," cut in Kenyon, "but that's not the place to start hunting. Down yonder, from the lake and all the way to the west. That's where she might have wandered."

Slocum frowned. Kenyon did his best to lead the search away from the hidden mine. Slocum had never mentioned it, wanting to see how the marshal and the others responded if they came across it. But Elias Kenyon made a point of getting them back to the lakeshore and off the hillside where they might come across the opening.

Going along with it, Slocum began the search for the missing woman hundreds of yards from where Polly had vanished. He knew she had not simply wandered off. Why would she scream if she had? And if she had fallen into a deep crevice, he would have found her quickly. Someone had kidnapped her; that was the only explanation Slocum could come up with. It began to look as if Elias Kenyon knew more about it than he let on.

"Wallings and Kenyon," Slocum muttered to himself.

"What's that, Slocum?" the marshal asked.

"I wonder about Kenyon. And his partner. Where do he and Ash Wallings get their money? I heard a barkeep say they were miners, but they always seem to be in Corinne."

"Miners? Could be. Never much thought on it before. They keep their noses clean and don't cause trouble." The marshal glanced at Slocum. "You thinkin' Wallings had something to do with Miss Greene's disappearance?"

"Just speculating on where the two get their money. If they're miners, what claim do they work?"

"I don't rightly know, but they seem to get into a few

high stakes games. Why, Ash Wallings lost damned near five hundred dollars not long ago.''

''A powerful lot to lose if you don't have a job,'' Slocum observed.

''Maybe they are miners. They aren't robbers. I keep an ear to the ground for stage or railroad robberies,'' the marshal said. ''Haven't been any to speak of in more than a year. Not in these parts.''

Slocum believed the lawman. A robbery from the Union Pacific would bring with it a sizable reward. For a man getting no more than forty dollars a month for his job as marshal, a big reward could mean the difference between eating nothing but beans and having a steak on his plate now and again.

''The monster!'' cried Elias Kenyon. ''There, out in the water! See it?''

Everyone rushed to the edge of Bear Lake and looked, but no one else saw it. Slocum noted how uneasy the others in the posse became at the mention of the creature. Kenyon did his best to spook the others whenever he could—and he led them away from the opening to the mine.

An idea began forming in Slocum's head about what had transpired around the banks of Bear Lake. Holes still filled the fabric, but he thought he understood enough now. With that knowledge, he ought to be able to find Polly Greene quickly enough.

''Marshal, are Beckwourth and Lawton having any luck selling their mine?'' Slocum spoke loud enough for Elias Kenyon to overhear. ''I heard tell a couple more buyers from California were on their way to look over the Lovely Lady.''

''Haven't heard anything on that, Slocum,'' the marshal said. The lawman turned and squinted at Slocum. ''You're not thinkin' on givin' them any woe on that, are you? You never tole me why you was tellin' folks you represented buyers back in New Orleans.''

''Just passing the time,'' Slocum lied. He watched Kenyon's face turn white when he added, "But these gents are rolling in money. Heard tell they own a dozen mines in Nevada and want to move into Utah. Money's no object."

"So tell Beckwourth and Gold Tooth," the marshal said. "We got a woman to find, and it's gettin' danged hot out here." The lawman wiped his face with his bandanna before moving on along the lake to join three others. Two more ranged ahead. Slocum held back and watched Elias Kenyon.

The man shifted from foot to foot, obviously unsettled by the news of new buyers for the Lovely Lady. When he thought no one noticed, Elias Kenyon moved uphill into a thicket. For several seconds he waited there. When no one called to him, he plunged into the undergrowth and bulled his way uphill, lighting out like a scalded dog.

Slocum followed at a more leisurely pace. Kenyon made no effort to hide his trail. He obviously considered speed more important than concealment. As Slocum slowly realized Kenyon's route was taking him back to the mine facing Bear Lake, he smiled.

He had beat the bushes and flushed the man responsible for Polly Greene's kidnapping. Now all he needed to do was let Elias Kenyon take him straight to her.

Slocum reached the worn path through the forest and knew Kenyon had run directly to the hidden mine opening. Slocum paused for a moment, considering how best to approach. Then he moved off the path and worked his way through the underbrush as quietly as possible.

Once, he caught sight of Kenyon. Slocum ducked behind a low-growing piñon and waited a few minutes, then continued his sneak toward the mine. He didn't want to set the man running before he led Slocum to Polly's side. As he rose to see if anyone was around the mouth of the mine, Slocum heard a footstep behind him. His hand flashed for his gun. He had his six-shooter half drawn when a heavy branch crashed into his skull. He tumbled to the ground, knocked out colder than a dead fish.

16

Light danced across Slocum's closed eyes. He winced at the pain in the back of his skull but didn't open his eyes all the way. Chancing a small slit, he tried to make heads or tails of his location. Twisting slightly convinced him he was tied up, hands bound behind his back. A kick or two showed him his ankles were similarly bound. Only then did he open his eyes more than a crack.

He groaned when he saw he was again in Tork Beckwourth and Gold Tooth Lawton's powder shed.

The door stood open a few inches, and out in the bright sunlight the two miners argued again. This time Joe Haskell wasn't around to keep them from coming to blows. Beckwourth swung on his partner and landed a clumsy blow to the top of the other man's head. Lawton staggered back, grabbed his skull, then roared like a wounded bull and charged. He collided squarely with Beckwourth before the larger man could launch another of his haymakers.

Knowing the fight couldn't last forever, Slocum swung about and sat up. He sucked in his breath and held it when pain rocketed through him. The dizziness passed quickly, but his arms were cold and numb from being cramped and tied under him for so long. He couldn't tell what time it was, but he guessed it to be late afternoon from the shadows. He had been out cold for several hours.

Rubbing the hemp rope against the side of a crate proved to be slow, tedious work, but he felt strand after strand giving way. He sawed faster when he heard the two miners end their fight. Slocum doubted they would shake hands, not after the way they fought so, but any truce meant disaster for him.

The heavy footsteps coming toward the powder shed told him they'd be inside before he could finish cutting himself free. Slocum slumped to the side and feigned unconsciousness once more.

"The little feller is still out, Gold Tooth," said Beckwourth. "I reckon I whumped him harder 'n I thought."

"You like to broke his damnfool neck, you big galoot."

Slocum took all this in—and tried to keep from sneezing. The two miners had carelessly spilled black blasting powder on the floor. He lay with his nose almost in a mound. Every breath, no matter how shallow, tickled his nose and made him want to sneeze.

Unable to restrain himself, Slocum let out a huge sneeze.

"Hey, he's awake. Men I put down with an axe handle don't sneeze when they get a snootful of powder." Tork Beckwourth kicked Slocum in the ribs. The pain forced him to open his eyes. Slocum glared at the towering miner, wondering what kind of death would be fitting.

Try as he might, Slocum couldn't think of one. Even the Apaches couldn't.

"What we gonna do with him?" demanded Gold Tooth Lawton. His front tooth shone like a beacon in the bright Utah sun. "He's done wrung us out one time too many."

"We kin always toss him into the lake. Trussed up like he is, he'd sink straight to the bottom." Beckwourth crossed his loglike arms on his chest and glared at Slocum.

"What do you have against me?" Slocum asked. He forced himself back to a sitting position and slowly worked against the ropes, hoping the miners wouldn't notice the small movement. Getting his hands free would help, but with his feet still hog-tied the way they were, he didn't stand a chance against these two.

"Danged near everything," Lawton declared. "You upped and killed Joe Haskell, just when we needed the varmint most."

"I didn't kill Haskell," said Slocum. "The judge threw out the charges against me."

"Jist 'cuz the judge didn't say you're guilty don't mean that you ain't," said Beckwourth. "The judge is a fool, and everybody in Corinne knows it. Him and that good-for-nothing boy of his."

"I didn't kill Haskell, though I had reason after he tried to trap me in your mine."

"What's that?" Lawton squinted curiously at Slocum. "What are you saying?"

"I was in the Lovely Lady, just taking a look around, thinking maybe I ought to make an offer," Slocum lied, "and Haskell tossed in a stick of dynamite. Collapsed the mine on me. I was lucky to get out."

"Haskell'd never do a stupid thing like that," Lawton said. "He needed the commission we promised if he could unload the mine. Nobody'd buy a collapsed mine shaft."

"Then one of you tried to kill me," Slocum said. "This is your property, so it had to be either you or Beckwourth."

The two miners looked at each other. The bafflement convinced Slocum neither had tried to sabotage their own mine with him inside.

But who had done it? Again, Slocum's thoughts turned in other directions. More pieces of the puzzle fell into place, but he still needed a few facts before being sure.

"Ain't either of us," Beckwourth finally said. "You're jist tryin' to keep us from gettin' rid of your carcass."

"So feed me to your monster," Slocum shot back.

The men's expressions startled Slocum, but not too much.

"That's one reason we want away from this goldurned mine," Lawton said. "We don't want no part of a monster living out there in the lake. No, sir, we don't."

"I kin rassle any critter on the face of the earth, be it bear or man, but I want nothin' to do with the monster," Beckwourth said uneasily. His eyes darted from side to side as if the creature in the lake might be creeping up on him. The fear etched onto the miners' faces was too real to be pretense. Slocum had to believe the pair feared the monster as much as they did anything else on the face of the earth.

Slocum had no chance to pursue the dread in the miners. Tork Beckwourth came over and took out his frustration on Slocum by kicking him hard in the side. Slocum sagged back, his ropes still not yielding. Before Beckwourth could swing a heavy boot at him again, Gold Tooth Lawton grabbed his partner's arm and yanked hard.

"We got to decide what to do with him. Now, Tork, we got to do it *now*. I want to toss him into the lake."

"What? Carry him all the way over the mountain? You do it. I'm not carryin' this varmint one inch more!"

"You dragged him here from the lake," protested Lawton. "He's the root cause of all our woe. We got to do something with him."

"Let's set him on a keg of powder and blow him to hell and gone," suggested Beckwourth.

"Waste our powder? It costs money. Why not just up and shotgun the bastard?" Gold Tooth Lawton shoved out his chin in a belligerent fashion that itched to be hit.

Tork Beckwourth could not restrain himself. He hauled off and clipped his partner on the chin, sending Lawton staggering away.

"You come up with dumb notions. If 'n we got to get rid of him—and we do, if we want to sell this miserable pit— come up with a good idea. Not them stupid ideas you—"

Beckwourth grunted and staggered back when Lawton swung a haymaker. It didn't connect squarely, but even a glancing blow was enough to send the giant miner to the ground. He snarled and jumped to his feet, grabbing Lawton in a grip intended to break any man's back.

Slocum lost sight of the two battling miners and knew he had only a few minutes. They were intent on getting rid of him. He didn't bother sitting up again. He found a nail poking out of a crate and used the head to worry away the last few strands of rope binding him. Even after the rope parted, Slocum lay still, letting the circulation return painfully to his numb hands. Only when he was sure he could use his fingers did he attack the ropes around his ankles. He ripped off the last of the rope and stood on shaky legs.

Peering out, he saw Beckwourth and Lawton rolling over and over in the dirt. He shook his head. He didn't understand the two men. They spent as much time punching each other as they did working their claim, even if it was a poor one.

He touched his empty holster, wondering where they had put his Colt Navy and rifle. The ramshackle cabin looked as good a place as any. Slocum simply walked down to it, paying no attention to the struggling men. In their all-out fight, they didn't see that their prisoner had freed himself. Slocum smiled when he glanced into the cabin. On the shaky table in the center of the room lay his six-shooter and rifle. He grabbed them, checking to be sure they were both loaded.

Slocum considered taking the rifle and putting both men out of their misery, but the last of the mystery had fallen into place for him, seeing both miners' reaction to the simple mention of the Bear Lake monster. Tork Beckwourth and Gold Tooth Lawton might be miserable human beings, but they weren't Slocum's enemies, even though they argued over how best to get rid of him.

Slocum headed up the side of the hill, struggling in the loose shale. He reached the trees and turned back to see the two miners had finished their battle. Beckwourth pointed up the hill and yelled incoherently. Gold Tooth Lawton grabbed for their shotgun and leveled it. Slocum judged the distance and knew he wasn't likely to be in any danger. When only one barrel of the double-barreled shotgun fired, he still ducked. But the shot fell far short.

Wasting no more time, Slocum began trudging up the hill, intent on reaching the other side and finding the marshal and the posse hunting for Polly Greene. Slocum might not know where the woman was, but he knew who had kidnapped her.

He even thought he knew what was going on around Bear Lake—and Professor Malloy would not like it one bit.

Slocum reached the top of the ridge, out of breath. It took a few seconds for him to get his bearings. Checking the sun, he knew he had only an hour until sundown. The evening winds already kicked up and blew off the lake, carrying a hint of chill that warned Slocum time might be running out if he intended to free Polly. His fingers tapped the butt of his six-gun, and he knew there would be shooting before this was over.

Those who deserved it would end up with a few slugs in their bellies.

Slipping and sliding in his haste, Slocum made his way down the hillside and finally reached Bear Lake's shoreline. The sun dipped behind a tall peak, cutting off light. Twilight was no time to be tracking the posse, but Slocum had no good idea how to locate the marshal and those with him. He might fire a shot and wait to see who answered, but he wanted to stay ahead of the two miners from the Lovely Lady Mine. Beckwourth and Lawton still had it in their heads he was their foe.

Slocum wasted no time starting for the hidden mine he had discovered. In it lay the key to releasing Polly Greene. The marshal might be in this direction, led astray by Elias Kenyon, but Slocum wasn't counting on it. He had failed to track Kenyon before. He wasn't going to be waylaid twice.

For Polly's sake, he dared not.

Slocum trudged along, reaching the base of the peninsula jutting out into the lake. At the tip of it lay the cave Professor Malloy thought was the monster's lair. Slocum smiled crookedly. He passed the far side of the peninsula and went into the cove where he had shot at the monster. He started for the worn trail leading to the hidden mine when he heard something moving ahead of him.

Dropping to one knee, Slocum raised his rifle and called out, "Move a muscle and I'll kill you! Get out where I can see you."

"Don't shoot!" came a frightened voice. Gold Tooth Lawton came from the undergrowth, hands held high. "You got no call to gun me down!"

Slocum tried not to laugh. "You and your partner tried to kill me twice," he said. But as he spoke, the hairs rippled on the back of his neck.

Slocum ducked, pulling the rifle from his shoulder and driving the butt straight back as hard as he could. The wood stock crunched into Tork Beckwourth's knee, causing the giant to yelp in pain.

Slocum kept swinging, moving clumsily along the muddy shoreline. The rifle went up in a wide arc and landed hard on Beckwourth's shoulder, sending the giant miner staggering into the water. This gave Slocum time to get to his feet.

Beckwourth fell heavily into the lake, but as he stumbled, he grabbed the rifle barrel and yanked it from Slocum's grip. Releasing it, Slocum watched the miner sink into the water, sputtering for breath. His hand went to his Colt Navy—but he had forgotten Lawton.

"Reach for that hogleg and I'll blow your head off," Lawton said. Slocum cast a quick look over his shoulder and saw the miner standing ten feet away, the long-barreled shotgun leveled at him.

"I'm not the one causing you trouble," Slocum tried to explain.

"We know what's goin' on," Lawton said. "You kilt Haskell. We needed that snake oil salesman something fierce. Nobody'll believe us when we try to sell the worthless mine. We *needed* him and his silver tongued ways and you upped and shot him in the back. And you used *my* shotgun!"

Slocum considered throwing down on the miner. He didn't have much hope of making it. Buckshot traveled faster than his hand could grab iron. And making the situation worse, Tork Beckwourth struggled wet and bedraggled from the lake.

The giant miner shook like a dog, sending water droplets in all directions. He growled deep in his throat as he waded ashore.

"No more arguin' over how to get rid of him. I'll break his neck!" Beckwourth held out his hands and moved for Slocum.

Slocum knew he had no alternative. He had to draw and shoot, Lawton first and then Tork Beckwourth.

Before he could reach for his Colt, a familiar mournful foghorn bellow echoed across the lake. Slocum turned and stared past the lumbering miner. At the edge of the cove loomed a dark shape, writhing about sinuously and moving in their direction.

"The monster!" Lawton cried. "The monster's gonna et us for sure!" He fired his shotgun. Both barrels·sent their leaden charge sailing into the night. The monster barely reacted.

The creature wailed again and came straight for them.

17

Beckwourth and Lawton let out whoops of stark terror and took off running as fast as they could go. Beckwourth made sucking noises as he fled and Lawton's boots crashed heavily into the brush, but both vanished into the undergrowth before Slocum could react. He stared at the approaching monster, deafened by the beastly wailing. He slowly drew his six-shooter and cocked it.

Slocum stopped when he leveled the gun. The monster changed course and headed back into the lake. Lowering his six-gun, Slocum watched carefully. The surprise at seeing the shadowy creature appear so suddenly subsided. Unlike the two miners, Slocum felt no fear. He holstered his six-shooter, knowing he could never bring down such a huge creature. Looking for his rifle, Slocum finally found it half buried in the muddy bank of Bear Lake.

He wiped off the mud, made sure the barrel was clear, then lifted it to his shoulder for a shot at the monster. As his finger tightened on the trigger, the dark silhouette vanished from the cove and into the lake. Slocum relaxed and lowered the rifle.

The mournful yowling came again, a sound combining sorrow and fear and outright pain in its trembling notes. Then the monster disappeared entirely from sight. Slocum took out after it, hurrying around the cove to reach the far side. From that vantage, he reckoned he could see it all the way across the lake. The distance was short, but it took Slocum longer than he thought.

Dense undergrowth tangled his feet, and the lengthening shadows turned to inky darkness, making the going even harder. When he reached the far shore, the monster had vanished completely. Slocum crouched on the bank and carefully scanned the lake for any ripple, any trace that the creature had passed this way. He saw nothing.

Twisting at a new cry, Slocum swung his rifle up and then stopped. He saw another inlet a half mile around the lake; this held his attention. The monster's cries came from that cove. Slocum bent and studied the shoreline and saw evidence that a small boat had been beached there recently. The gentle wave action of the lake water had yet to erase it. Feeling the weight of time pressing down heavily on him, Slocum trotted along the shore, preferring to stay just in the water rather than fight through the tangled undergrowth.

He stopped and stared into the cove where the monster's cries had come from. He couldn't make out much, but a curious pair of rocky knife blades rose from the water. Drawn by the peculiar rock formation, Slocum edged around and shoved himself into the crevice between them. As he moved, he scraped his rifle stock against one stony wall. An echo rattled forth and drifted over the lake, sounding as if someone had ripped the soul from a damned human.

Startled, Slocum waited for the echoes to die. Somehow, the formation of rock channeled the sound, magnified it, and sent it across the lake. He pushed deeper into the crevice and saw a stool. He turned and sat on it. From this position he had a fair view of the lake—and immediately under the stool lay a battered army bugle.

"Never was much good," Slocum said, picking up the

instrument. He put it to his lips and let out a hearty puff of wind. A choking noise rolled along the crevice and across the lake. A second try produced a better sound, one matching the melancholy cry of the Bear Lake monster. Slocum took a deep breath and blew again. The echoes in the crevice threatened to rob him of hearing, so he put down the bugle.

He had seen enough. Someone—and it wasn't any monster on the lake—produced the sounds people had been hearing for going on six months. From this vantage, a man could be sure no one rowed on the lake before emitting the cry. Or he could be certain someone *was* on the lake.

Slocum knew this would frighten away fishermen and anyone else using the lake for transport. The unusual rock formation amplified sounds so that a simple blast could be heard for miles.

"One mystery solved," Slocum said. "Another to go." He paused as he stood, climbing onto the stool. He had two more mysteries to unravel. The important one dealt with Polly's whereabouts. Getting his balance, he reached up and found an iron spike driven into the rock. Using the stool and this spike, Slocum pulled himself up. Holes and other spikes provided an easy way to clamber to the top of the formation.

A sudden gust of wind almost took off his hat. Slocum pulled his Stetson down firmly and swung around. From atop the rock cleavers, he had a perfect view of the lake, including the first cover where he had taken a shot at the monster. Beyond that cove stretched the dark finger of land jutting into the lake—where Professor Malloy thought the monster laired.

Slocum now had other ideas. There wasn't a monster other than the one Elias Kenyon and Ash Wallings had created to frighten everyone. They were the ones in Corinne who had done the most to spread the wild rumors about the monster. They must have made sure the parson heard their bugling and the schoolmarm, also. Slocum imagined the pleasure the two took in frightening her. Miss Smith, the boy in town had named her.

If their reason for the charade wasn't obvious, their methods were. Slocum stared down into another inlet along Bear Lake's shore and saw the monster.

He had to relax. His hand actually touched the butt of his six-shooter before he realized what the monster truly was.

"Sailcloth. A wood frame. And a rowboat." Slocum saw the clever bracing and way the two men had fashioned their cutout creature. One sat on the stool below, blowing away with the monster's lamentations, while the other rowed in the boat with the large silhouette showing to any on the shore who might happen along.

From his vantage, Slocum slowly turned and studied the terrain, hoping to catch sight of the marshal and the posse with him. The wind blew through the tall trees creating the only movement he saw. Changing his stance, he stared back in the direction of Professor Malloy's camp, wondering if the scholar stood watch with his spyglass. Slocum waved a few times, then gave up the effort. Even if Malloy sighted him, he might not make out who signaled. And in no case would the professor understand what Slocum wanted.

"I'm on my own. Let's hope I'm quick enough, Polly," Slocum muttered to himself. He stared at the crude ladder leading back to the stool and bugle. He had no reason to go there. Walking along the precarious edge of the rocky ledge, he came to a rope ladder tossed down the sheer face of a stony cliff. Slocum wasted no time in hurrying down, though he was an exposed target the entire way. He counted on the dark hiding him as it had the perpetrators of this cruel hoax.

Jumping the last few feet, Slocum dropped into a crouch. Not five yards distant, the rowboat was beached. Leaning against a rocky wall stood the fake monster. He went to it and saw how Wallings and Kenyon had fixed it so it would float behind the rowboat as one of them rowed out. No one would notice the boat if they saw the creature.

From the way they had rigged it with inflated animal bladders, they might even be able to let it sink into the water, as a reptile might dive for the bottom of the lake. Slocum had to admire their handiwork, even if he didn't understand it.

Yet.

The shore here was muddy and was filled with tracks showing how several people had come and gone repeatedly. When Slocum saw a smaller footprint, his heart leaped.

Polly! He drew his Colt and advanced more rapidly. He didn't want her in those owlhoots' clutches for even another minute. The tracks led into a dark cave, possibly flooded if the spring runoff lifted the level of the lake more than a foot or two, but now, it was filled with only a few inches of water. Slocum started in, every sense straining.

The blackness dropped around him like a shroud. After a few paces, he couldn't tell front from back. Placing his left hand against one slimy wall, he glanced over his shoulder. The mouth of the cave gave only a dim hint of where he had entered.

Although he wished he had more light, Slocum knew he could not back away now. His every instinct screamed that Polly was being held prisoner here.

He went a few yards deeper into the cave, the only sound reaching his ears the steady drip, drip, drip of water from the cave roof. It pattered against the brim of his hat, into his face, and over his gun hand. Slocum kept moving deeper.

When his left hand lost the wall, he almost panicked. Then he realized a branch went off in that direction. Risking the element of surprise, Slocum softly called, "Polly? Are you here? Make a noise if you can hear me."

For a moment the only sound he heard was the thudding of his own heart. Then came a frantic scratching from ahead. Slocum penetrated deeper into the cave and almost fell over the bound and gagged woman.

"Polly!" He dropped down and felt the body he had stumbled over. She moaned and wiggled and made loud, angry sounds through the cloth shoved into her mouth.

Slocum pulled it out and got a torrent of incomprehensible words.

"Whoa, slow down. Not so fast."

"John, thank heaven it is you! Wallings. Wallings and his partner. I don't know his name—"

"Elias Kenyon," Slocum supplied, working on the woman's ropes. Her captors had bound her cruelly tight. Even after he had freed her, she was unable to flex her fingers. He rubbed life back into them, then she clung to him with savage desperation.

"It was horrible here in the dark. I don't know what they were going to do."

Slocum didn't bother telling her his suspicions. Polly was lucky to still be alive. If it hadn't been for the marshal and posse hunting for her, she might have been dead long before now.

"We can get out of here right now. All I need to do is retrace my path in. Can you walk?"

"I'll crawl if I have to," she said fervently. Polly hugged him again and awkwardly kissed him in the almost complete darkness.

"Want me to light a lucifer?"

"It might be nice," Polly said, "but I've been in the dark forever! I'm afraid it might blind me. I'd rather blunder along until we are outside." She clung to his arm. "John, thank you for rescuing me."

"It's night out. They've had you for quite a spell. You know Wallings and Kenyon created the monster. It's nothing but the wood and cloth outline of some sea serpent. And they made the monster cry using an old army bugle."

"I thought as much. They never spoke much in my presence, but I got the impression they were perpetrating a hoax on the residents around Bear Lake.''

"Any idea why?" Slocum asked. The more he thought on it, the more sure he was of the answer. He needed confirmation of what was only a guess.

"No, I—John, look out!" Polly shoved him hard. Slocum fell facedown into the water, his six-shooter thrust out in front of him.

The foot-long lance of fire leaping at him from the mouth of the cave blinded him. Polly had been in the cave longer and her eyes had adjusted to almost absolute darkness, allowing her to see movement when he did not. But his reactions were good. Slocum fired a round in the direction of the bushwhacker and was rewarded with a yelp as hot lead found its mark.

"You winged me, you son of a bitch. This time I'm gonna kill you dead!" Slocum recognized Ash Wallings's voice.

"I'm sorry I didn't put you out of your misery before, you sidewinder," Slocum called. He knew he hadn't seriously hurt Wallings this time. At best, he might have sent a few rock chips flying into the man's face.

Getting out of the water, Slocum pushed Polly back into the cave. Huddled along one wall, he whispered to her, "Is there any other way out of the cave? Wallings has us bottled up."

"There must be, John. I heard strange noises more than once. And I don't think they used this tunnel after they brought me in."

"It's probably too exposed for their liking. Anyone outside hunting along the bank or rowing on the lake might see them come and go and get suspicious. I reckon they store the parts of their monster just inside the cave so no one will see it during the day."

Slocum ducked when Ash Wallings fired twice down the tunnel. The bullets danced off the narrow walls and ricochetted around behind him. Slocum protected Polly the best he could, but he knew they weren't going to get out of this alive unless Ash Wallings got mighty careless.

"You meddled enough where you didn't belong, Slocum," called Wallings from safely outside the cave. "I'm sorry I didn't plug you when I had the chance. You talkin' around Corinne about the monster made folks suspicious."

"You wanted them scared, didn't you?" Slocum called back. He had to keep Wallings talking until he either made a mistake or Slocum figured some way out of their predicament. His Colt Navy had only four rounds left. He didn't rightly remember what he had done with his rifle, not that it mattered too much. After Tork Beckwourth had thrown it into the lake, Slocum didn't much trust it.

Right now, though, the chance of it blowing up in his hands seemed less dangerous than getting drilled by Ash Wallings.

"Down there," Slocum said, shoving Polly down the tunnel to the left of where he had accidentally found on his way in. The right-angle bend provided some protection against the occasional slugs Wallings sent winging after them.

"This might be the way they came into the cave," Polly said, excited. "I'll see if I can find the exit." She slipped from his wet hands before he could stop her. In the darkness, she might fall into a hole and be lost forever. Slocum chanced a quick look around the corner and saw Wallings's faint outline. Slocum fired twice, hitting the man both times, but some instinct kept Slocum where he was.

Then he saw that the body didn't drop as it should have if he had really hit Wallings. The light wasn't too good, but Slocum finally made out the ragged edges of sailcloth strung over a wooden cross. Wallings had tried to dupe him. Slocum cursed. He had wasted two bullets on a phony target. Wallings and his partner had gotten too good with their monster.

"John," came Polly's excited cry. "I think I've found it. A way out. There's a ladder going up. And boxes. I found their supplies!"

Slocum cautiously made his way toward the sound of her

voice. He hesitated to light a lucifer, yet he had to if he wanted to see what Polly had found. He wasn't going to plunge headlong into a trap just because he couldn't see.

"Cover your eyes," he cautioned. It took Slocum several tries to get a lucifer from its metal container. When it flared, he squinted. In the guttering flame Slocum saw the supplies the two bushwhackers had stored: mostly food and other items worthless to help him and Polly escape. But the woman had been right about something more important.

A rope ladder dangled down at the far corner of the room. It vanished into a black circle in the ceiling. Slocum saw no reason for them to string up a ladder unless it went somewhere—such as to the surface.

"Go on up," Slocum urged. "I'll hold it steady for you." When Polly started up, as she would climb an ordinary ladder, the contraption swung away from Slocum.

"Put one foot on either side and go up that way," he told her. He burned his fingers as the lucifer died down. His vision consisted of dancing blue and yellow dots for a few seconds and he had to work by feel. He touched her leg and felt her recoil from him.

"Go on, hurry," he told her. Slocum had the feeling that Wallings had tired of waiting and was coming after them. He had to know the cave far better than Slocum. To get trapped here spelled immediate death.

"I see stars above, John. It does lead out!"

"Climb!"

Slocum followed quickly. Polly tumbled out of the top of the long shaft. Slocum traversed the thirty feet to the surface and spilled out after her, rolling over and poking his Colt Navy down into the shaft, ready to shoot Ash Wallings if he showed his head.

"Just you stay on your belly, Slocum," came Elias Kenyon's cold voice. "Move a muscle and I'll blow your head off."

18

"You jist shove that six-gun of yours to one side," Kenyon ordered. "And stay on your belly where you belong, you low-down snake. You done caused us enough grief."

Slocum wondered at Elias Kenyon. The man made the same accusation against him as Tork Beckwourth.

"What have I done to cause you any trouble?" Slocum had to ask.

"You been goin' around gettin' people to study the monster, to come lookin' for it. We want everyone to be *a-feared* of it!"

"The professor—" Polly began.

"You shut your tater trap, too, missy," Kenyon said. "There's a powerful lot of decidin' me and Wallings got to do." The man shouted to his partner to get up to the top of the cliff overlooking the small cove where they had launched their fake monster. It took Ash Wallings several minutes to reach the top. Every second of delay caused Slocum to fume even more.

"Why didn't you just pull the trigger, Kenyon?" Wallings demanded. "We want them both dead. They're too much trouble alive."

"Why did we keep the woman alive for so long?" Kenyon

asked, as if speaking to a small child. He answered his own question. "We did it 'cuz the marshal and a whole danged posse came out here nosin' around. The jig would be up for us if they found her body all mauled by the monster."

"Like you killed Dark Cloud?" Slocum rolled to one side to watch the faces of the two men. The way their lips curled told Slocum he had found the Paiute's killers.

"That we did. We got a haying fork and used it on him. Sharpened the tines down real good and jist gutted the poor red bastard. Never knew what struck him."

"You were the ones who tossed the dynamite into the Lovely Lady and trapped me, weren't you?"

"Reckon so," Wallings said, grinning now in recollection. "You're a hard man to kill."

"I don't understand," Polly said. "Why are you doing this? It's horrible!"

"They're stealing ore that rightly belongs to Beckwourth and Lawton," Slocum said. "They burrowed in from this side of the mountain, but my reading of the Lovely Lady's claim shows Beckwourth and Lawton own all the land over the top of the hill and down to Bear Lake."

"That's right, Slocum," Kenyon agreed. "We been diggin' out their gold for almost two years. Can't rightly tell anyone we struck it rich 'cuz it all belongs to those worthless miners. Beckwourth and Lawton couldn't find gold if it fell from the sky and hit them on the head."

"That nugget Mr. Beckwourth had. He must have found it and—"

"No, Polly, it wasn't like that," Slocum said. "Beckwourth hired Joe Haskell to sell the mine for him. That fake nugget was part of the fraud to make potential buyers think the Lovely Lady was worth more than it was. Any good mining engineer could glance at the ore coming from the mine and know different."

"We tried scarin' off everyone so's Beckwourth and ol' Gold Tooth couldn't sell."

"A new owner might dig deeper and find where you had been high-grading their ore," Slocum said. "The least a corporation buying the land would do is order a new survey of the property. That would uncover your mine, wouldn't it?"

"You're gettin' the idea why we got to make the monster kill you two," Kenyon said.

"Can't do that," complained Wallings. "Two more? That will get the marshal out of his soft chair for sure. If too many die, the whole town will feel threatened and demand something be done. The girl, go on. It's only right, the trouble she and that old geezer with her brought down on our heads. But if Slocum's et by the monster too, that'll be too much to bear."

"Too many people have been dying out here," Slocum pointed out. "You killed Haskell, didn't you, Kenyon?"

"That was Wallings's doing," the miner snapped. "He couldn't even aim that danged shotgun of Tork Beckwourth's right."

"It misfired. I had him dead to rights and the shell didn't fire right." Wallings rubbed his belly where Slocum had hit him after the unsuccessful bushwhacking back in Corinne. From the way he moved, Slocum realized he hadn't hurt the man seriously.

"Why'd you open up on me in town?" Slocum asked.

"Had to get rid of you. Poke around too much and people would know we made up the monster. We read that fine article in the *Deseret News* a spell back and the idea came to us it was a good way to frighten off folks. Took some doing to get the monster just right," bragged Elias Kenyon.

"There's no creature in the lake?" Polly sounded crushed. Slocum wished she would think a bit harder and realize her life was perilously close to ending because of the damned Bear Lake monster.

"Only what we showed folks," Wallings said. "But what are we going to do, Kenyon? I say, bury Slocum somewhere. Bury 'im alive, if you want. I'd like to do that—do the job right this time. But no more killings from the monster. After her, that is."

"Both," Kenyon said. "I enjoyed ripping the guts out of that Injun. Two more deaths will scare everybody away from our mine."

"Why don't you buy out Beckwourth and Lawton?" Polly asked. "You have the money from your illicit mining. That would make you the legal owners."

Both miners stared at her. "We never thought of that," admitted Wallings.

"Wouldn't work," Kenyon rushed on. "Questions would get asked. We've killed too many people for the sale to go through without them finding out."

"Might be true," Wallings said, willing to be convinced. "Besides, why pay for something we're gettin' for free, anyway?"

"Right," Kenyon agreed.

Slocum inched toward his six-shooter, but Kenyon saw and moved to cut him off. Kenyon shoved the gun into his belt. "You stay there, Slocum. We'll be finished with you soon enough."

"It'll be daylight before you know it," Wallings pointed out. "You want to kill her now and let her body wash out into the lake so's she can be found?"

"It's time to do it. We been actin' like cowards. We need to get back to minin', not prancin' around and wastin' all our time foolin' with the monster." Elias Kenyon grabbed Polly by the scruff of the neck and pulled the blond to her feet. "You get on down the hill. Come this way. No need to go to the cove."

"John!" She reached out to Slocum, but Kenyon shoved her from Slocum's sight. Slocum surged, ready to jump to his feet and stop Kenyon. A hard barrel landed alongside his head, stunning him.

Wallings stepped back and said, "Kenyon's lettin' me do what I will with you, Slocum. Do you cotton to diggin' your own grave? That would amuse me." Ash Wallings prodded Slocum with the gun barrel and motioned him after Kenyon and Polly Greene.

Slocum stood, but he wobbled, weaving away and clutching his head. He tottered at the edge of the cliff. The inlet below swung around in wide circles as he twisted.

"What're you doin'?" Wallings stepped back, six-shooter leveled.

"My head. It's breaking apart. Can't stand it." Slocum started to fall over the cliff. Wallings reacted instinctively, grabbing for Slocum's arm.

Slocum dropped to one knee, clutching Wallings's wrist. Tugging hard, he got the miner off balance and staggering. Wallings screamed as he pitched over the edge of the cliff, falling thirty feet to the muddy shore below.

Slocum almost tumbled after Ash Wallings. He grabbed at rocks, dug his toes into the face of the cliff, did whatever he could to keep from plummeting after his foe. The dizziness had been feigned. His attempts to hang on weren't. Inch by inch, Slocum fought to get back onto the top of the cliff. Only when he stood on solid rock did he dare look down at Wallings. The man lay in a twisted heap on the ground. From the crazy angle of his neck, Wallings must have broken it in the fall.

"Good riddance," Slocum muttered. He spat over the cliff in Ash Wallings's direction. The wind caught the spittle and carried it away from the body. Slocum would have felt better killing Ash Wallings with his own hands, but this was good enough for the moment. And he still had Kenyon to find and eliminate.

Unarmed, Slocum took off after Elias Kenyon and Polly, careful not to go too fast. He didn't want to overtake them and have the miner plug him with his own six-shooter.

The trail from the top of the cliff was clear, but Slocum didn't see or hear either of the people ahead of him. Changing his mind, he broke into a run, throwing caution to the winds. He dared not let Polly stay with Kenyon an instant longer. The man wanted to do to her what he had already done to Dark Cloud.

Slocum reached the shoreline and looked around. To his left lay the cove with the fake monster and Ash Wallings's body. To his right came soft whimpering sounds.

"Polly!" He took off in that direction and almost immediately found Kenyon and his captive. He had her tied and advanced on her with a large haying fork, the three tines sharpened wickedly. Slocum saw then how Dark Cloud had died—and he had to keep Kenyon from killing Polly the same way.

"You!" Kenyon swung about, the sharp points thrusting at Slocum. Slocum danced back, looking for an advantage. He saw none. If Kenyon took it into his head to drop the haying fork, he need only draw the six-shooter at his side or Slocum's tucked in his belt and finish his killing.

Kenyon stabbed again at Slocum, but he was distracted when the monster vented its baleful cry.

"What's going on?" Kenyon turned and looked toward the two slabs of rock he had used to echo forth the fake monster's voice.

Slocum drove forward, fists swinging hard. One blow caught Kenyon on the side of the head and staggered him. Slocum's other fist smashed squarely into the man's gut, doubling him over. Grabbing the fork, Slocum wrenched it from Kenyon's grip. He took a step back, judged distances, and unloaded a powerful uppercut that snapped Kenyon's head up. The miner's eyes glazed over as he fell to the ground, knocked out.

"John, you stopped him." Polly struggled in her bonds.

Slocum hesitated in releasing her. He pulled his Colt Navy from Kenyon's belt and cocked it, pointing it at the unconscious man's head.

"John, no, don't. Don't lower yourself to his level. Don't murder him."

"After what he tried to do to you? What he and Wallings did to Dark Cloud and Haskell?" Slocum's grip was firm and his finger tightened on the trigger.

"There you are. Arrest that man, marshal. Do it now!" came Professor Hercules Malloy's voice. Slocum relaxed and let the hammer down gently on his six-shooter. The lawman bustled around and rolled Kenyon over onto his back.

"Heard some of what went on. He's the one what killed Haskell?"

"He is, marshal, he is! He confessed!" cried Polly. Slocum released the woman, and she clung to him fiercely, shaking in reaction to the closeness of her death. "He did all manner of terrible things. He even faked the creature in the lake!"

Slocum frowned. He stared at the professor and asked, "How'd the monster come to call out when he did? How'd *you* find us?"

"Why, Mr. Slocum, give me credit for some sense. I saw you much earlier waving in my direction. The marshal remained in our camp, though the others had returned to Corinne. It took us a spell to find you."

"You found the trumpet?"

"Alas, yes, and I used it to distract Kenyon," the professor admitted. "It is a shock to find there is no creature in Bear Lake."

"It's a relief to know I got the varmint causing all the trouble in these parts," the marshal said, pulling Kenyon upright. The man moaned softly but remained unconscious. The marshal turned to the professor and asked, "Does this mean I'll be gettin' the fifty dollar reward you promised for finding Miss Greene?"

"Of course, marshal. Here, here it is." Professor Malloy passed over fifty dollars. Slocum started to remind the professor he had already given the lawman fifty to form the posse. He held his tongue. The scholar had money to burn. Getting Polly Greene back unharmed was worth any amount of money.

Slocum quickly explained to the marshal what the two miners had been doing and finished, saying, "You can tell Beckwourth and Lawton they're rich men, that their mine finally paid off in spades."

"Rich men, the pair of 'em," marveled the marshal. "Who'd have thought it?" He cocked his head to one side and added, "Don't go expectin' either of them to thank you, Slocum. Not if what you say is true about them tryin' to kill you twice."

"It is," Slocum said, "but there's no need to press charges. You have the one responsible for the worst of the trouble around Bear Lake."

"I deny it all," moaned out Elias Kenyon. "It was all Wallings's doing. He made me do it all!"

"Cut his tongue out, marshal," suggested Slocum. "I'll do it for you, if you want."

"A moment, Mr. Slocum," broke in Professor Malloy. To Kenyon he addressed the question, "Why did you salt the monster's lair with broken eggs? Was it only part of your sham? And where did you get such large eggs?"

"What are you talkin' about?" Kenyon's eyes were clear now, but the expression on his face told Slocum the man wasn't lying. Not this time.

"Out on the peninsula. The creature's lair."

"We never been out there. No need. We done everything right out of this inlet where the cave gave us some cover."

"Get moving," the marshal said, shoving Kenyon ahead of him. Faint pinks lit the eastern horizon as the sun rose. "I want to get you in the hoosegow before noon. With luck, we can have a trial before sundown and stretch your neck tomorrow.

That'll save havin' to feed you more 'n a day or so.''

The marshal got his prisoner moving, and they soon disappeared around the bend in the lake.

"I don't understand," Polly said. "If Kenyon and Wallings didn't fake the lair, where—"

Slocum started to speak. Out on the lake, moving through a low-lying fog bank, he saw a large, rippling shape. Following it were two smaller bulges. He lifted his hand to point. A mournful cry rolled over the water, followed by shriller cries. The three lumps sank beneath the surface of Bear Lake, leaving only faint ripples behind.

"What was that?" Professor Malloy asked.

"I don't know," Slocum said slowly. "I really don't know." He took a deep breath and said, "Why don't we get back to Corinne? We can all use a hot meal, a bath, and a soft bed."

As they made their way along the lake, Slocum glanced back to the spot where he had seen the dark shapes moving so sinuously, but even the ripples were gone.